The Asphodels

The Asphodels

Carmen Bouldin

ISBN: 978-1-967407-07-1

Book Cover design: Jeanie A. Smith

Inside Cover design: Canva

Edgar Allan Poe poems, poetry quotes, or short story quotes used in this book are in the public domain: *Eldorado, To One in Paradise, The Raven, The Island of the Fay, The Gold-Bug, Eleonora, The Tell-Tale Heart, Bridal Ballad, Catholic Hymn, Morella, Berenice, Alone,* and *Spirits of the Dead.*

To Poe, with Love

Other works by Carmen Bouldin

Gothic Garden Series

The Rose Bush

Poetry

Eclectic Expressions

Recipe Books

*The Flavored Raven: Recipes Inspired from the Six Degrees
of Edgar Allan Poe*

Table of Contents

How does it feel to be named after death? I ask myself this question every day of my life. I do represent death! I was a surprise, an afterthought, after the birth of my twin sister, Astra. On April 29th, 1854, the midwife thought my mother was going to have a large baby; but little did she know, I was lurking behind my sister also waiting to be born.

As I was told by my father, Astra was born first. He said my mother beamed at the sight of her, for this was their first child. They anticipated having many more children in later years, just not as soon as this very day. He said that while my mother was holding my sister, she started having more pains. The midwife took the baby and handed her to an assistant, realizing a twin existed. In that fourth minute of my mother's pain, I arrived, the spitting image of my sister. Everyone was in shock. As soon as I sprang forth, my mother fainted and was bleeding profusely. Within ten minutes, she died, never holding her youngest daughter, never naming me. This task was left to a grieving man for his beloved dead wife, unable to fathom caring for two infant daughters and running a funerary business.

My father convinced the midwife, Lucia, to stay on and care for my sister and me for at least a few weeks until he could provide a governess for us. He also had a funeral to attend for my mother. Apparently, I was not named until after my mother's funeral. When my mother's coffin was lowered into the ground, my father admitted to looking around in our cemetery set against the backdrop of our home and my father's business. This is the first time he truly noticed all the asphodels growing around trees and tombstones adding an ethereal light to the darkness of death. At that moment, he named me: Asphodel.

He dashed into the house to hold my sister and me, promising to love us and provide for us for the rest of our lives. With a wailing waterfall of tears, he looked at Astra and said, "Astra, my first born, you are the light within your mother's eye who would have held you so dear. The astra was her favorite flower from which you were named." Turning to me, he said, "Asphodel, my second born, you are the light in my eye. I never knew a flower could be so beautiful and meaningful in death. Your mother would have loved you so."

He hugged us both, handing us to Lucia who brought us into the world and who would be our guiding light for the future.

Chapter 1

When Astra and I were in our youthful years of schooling, Madame Lucia, guided us in our studies: Latin, French, Mythology, History, reading, writing, and mathematics. On one occasion, we were studying the myth surrounding Persephone being taken into the Underworld by Hades. She was picking flowers, most likely narcissus, as she was kidnapped. I thought, "Maybe she was picking asphodels."

The unique part of this myth was the descriptions of Hekate allowing Persephone to move or transition between the world of the living and the dead. Hekate used the asphodels as a symbol of a torch to guide Persephone through.

This gave me hope that my name was not just a death flower. I could picture this myth in my mind where the stalk-like perennials stood tall with ghostly white petals touched with a tinge of pink shining brightly for Persephone to move between the seasons of time and space. It seemed almost as if she were appearing as a ghost each time she would cross the deathly plane into the human plane.

Learning about these myths mentioning asphodels, my name, brought me closer to the flowers themselves, but they also brought me closer to the cemetery where fields of asphodels grew each year from the beginning of spring in March to the end of spring in June. As a small child, I avoided the cemetery because I was afraid. I only went there if I was told we had to walk through it. Once I knew the mythology behind my flower, I was intrigued; thus, bringing me closer to the asphodel meadows throughout the tombstones. I was not frightened anymore. The asphodels brought me closer to the cemetery as well.

I began to tend to the flowers, which also allowed me to tend to the ground around each tombstone. Papa told me we had a groundskeeper for this sort of work, but I did not care. I wanted to be here working and thriving to keep the asphodels in their delightful state.

All of this began when I was around sixteen; however, now it was 1872, Astra and I were now eighteen with my father hoping we would both marry sooner rather than later. Astra was closer to that goal than I was to even think of that notion. I tended my asphodels and tombstones while Astra was attending parties and balls. She had a plethora of friends and was very popular with the society crowd. I, on the other hand, remained to myself at home or in the cemetery. My sister and I were exact opposites, explained by my father who told me I was like him and Astra was like my mother. I had no use for these parties and silly gatherings. I wanted to do something useful and contribute to our home.

Astra was vibrant wearing bold colors against her porcelain, soft skin unblemished from staying out of the sun. Her auburn hair was always worn partially up and the longer ringlets to one side complimented all of the gowns she wore. The dresses were always made of varying shades of green, teal, and aqua to bring out the green in her eyes. She was elegant, poised, and ever so loved by all. Some thought of her as a goddess torn from the pages of a Greek play. If they knew her as I did, they would see more of a tragedy than a comedy or drama. This is because she always blamed me for our mother's death. She told me once that I continually reminded her of this every time she saw me; moreover, I always thought this was illogical on her part. I knew she would always blame me, so I just ignored her. Unfortunately, since we were twins, I was the spitting image of Astra; however, my hair was always worn in a low chignon, my face was natural only slightly sun-kissed from the gardening I loved so much in the cemetery, and my dresses were always black or gray because at a young age I began to observe my father in the undertaking business since he did not have my mother anymore to help him. He wanted one of his children to learn the family business.

My father, Thomas Willoughby, began his working life as a cabinet maker, working extremely hard and becoming well known throughout the county with the business name, Willoughby Cabinetry. The needs of families grew to more than just cabinets, and so, he began making coffins during the Civil War. This quickly developed into an undertaking business where he and my mother, Belladonna, "undertook" all of the needs of families in mourning. They offered coffins, preparing the body for the wake in the home, carriages for carrying the family and the body to our cemetery, wailers, and the actual burial. They also sold mourning attire, memorial items, and flowers. When my mother died, it left my father to undertake all of this on his own, so he hired an assistant, which ended up being his cousin, Lucy McClemore. She was widowed during the civil war when her husband was shot in the head and died instantly. She moved in with us and assisted my father while Madame Lucia cared for Astra and myself, giving up her midwife duties to be a full-time governess until the end of our seventeenth year when she died of heart failure. Having both these ladies to help him allowed my father's business, now called Willoughby Undertakers after he moved into funeral services away from cabinet making, to grow and thrive throughout the community of Spencerton, VA.

I was ever so ecstatic to assist him since Cousin Lucy was getting on in age, unable to do as much as she could eighteen years ago. Surrounded by death and being named after a death flower created a melancholic persona I had no choice in accepting. My whole life was death, and it brought me peace helping others grieve through it. Astra had nothing to do with Papa's business, and never would. The lightness to the darkness, always in constant opposition. If only people knew the light half had more of a darker side than me.

Chapter 2

This morning, the house was buzzing because of a family coming in to bury their patriarch. The family, the Richardsons, moved to Spencerton about ten years ago. The patriarch, Guy De Vere Richardson, left a wife and a son, passing from a heart condition at the age of 58. The deceased's wife made an appointment with Papa to undertake the burial details. We were surprised Mrs. Richardson did not want us to pay a visit to her own home. Being a widow, she should not be seen so soon out in public after her husband's death, but she insisted she visit our home. We were expecting her at any time.

Papa liked me to greet our families because he felt the soft face of a woman eased their pain and suffering just slightly as they entered. I waited in the foyer so I could clearly hear Mrs. Richardson knock on the front door. Straightening odds and ends to pass the time moved quickly. The foyer was larger than many houses I have been in with dark hunter green walls. Two sconces lighted the entryway. The foyer was nothing fancy, but there was a small mahogany table where a vase always sat with fresh flowers. A large mirror donned the wall above the table. Anyone who entered would see their reflection.

Before I realized, fifteen minutes had passed bringing a soft knock at the door in twos. I opened the door gradually to reveal a lady. She carried herself confidently dressed in all black with the appropriate crepe donning her dress. A thin veil covered her face so I could just see the remnants of an aging beauty worn down with heavy eyes from tears for her beloved. Her golden hair was pinned in a bun where I could see small slivers of silver caressing her temples with pride. I stepped back from the door and welcomed her, "Good afternoon, please come in. My name is Asphodel Willoughby; my father will meet us in the parlor."

She stepped inside handing me her shawl. "Miss Willoughby, it is nice to make your acquaintance. I presume you are Mr. Willoughby's daughter?" she asked politely.

"Yes ma'am. I am one of his daughters. I have a twin sister, Astra, but she does not assist my father in his business. Only I do."

"Oh, how fascinating! So, you will be helping me along with your father; how lovely. Does anyone else help you two?"

"Yes ma'am, my dear cousin Lucy still assists us on occasion, but she has turned most of her duties over to me. We will explain everything during your appointment. We would have been ever so accommodating to come to your home to arrange the funeral details." I softly said.

"Oh dear, I appreciate the kindness, but I just had to get out of my house for just a little while. I know I should play the mourning rituals with prudence, but I have always played by my own rules. People may talk, but I am too old to care now." Mrs. Richardson added without compromise.

"Please follow me into the parlor. It is right this way." I offered out my hand politely, indicating the way to the parlor. For a smidge of a moment, I felt a slight bit confused why she would ask who all would be helping her; however, I dismissed the thought with not a care as we walked to the parlor.

My father was waiting for us. He was the average size man of the time with a height around 5'9". His hair had turned completely gray and he wore a mustache and beard. He appeared older than he actually was; however, if someone looked closely into his eyes, they would see the glimmer of youth still springing his steps.

As soon as Mrs. Richardson entered, Papa rose to his feet like a soldier with his commanding officer on arrival; he bowed welcoming her. "Mrs. Richardson, I am Thomas Willoughby, and I am so sorry for your loss. Asphodel and I want to make this process as seamless as possible to ease your grief. We want this time to be comforting to you as you remember your late husband."

"Thank you so much Mr. Willoughby," she said genuinely, putting her handkerchief to her eyes dabbing them delicately, "this was a shock to my family with the suddenness of his passing coming out the clear blue sky. He was not ill. He seemed as healthy as a horse."

My father gently asked, "To ensure I have the right spelling of your husband's name, could you spell it out for me please?"

"Yes, yes, his name was Guy De Vere Richardson. G-U-Y D-E V-E-R-E R-I-C-H-A-R-D-S-O-N."

"Thank you Madam."

"Mrs. Richardson, we are here for you in all your needs. Let me go check on the tea. Papa, I will return shortly." I added, hoping the tea would give her a little comfort; furthermore, truly hoping the tea would give her a distraction.

As I arrived into the kitchen, I noticed my sister was not present, even though she had promised to prepare the tea mix for our guest. "Winnie, have you seen Astra this morning?"

"Oh, yes'am. She came down to breakfast after you ate and left. She mixed a new blend of tea, then out the door she went. Said she had a meeting for lunch."

"So, she did mix the tea for us?" I nervously asked.

"She did indeed! It seems like it's going to be a nice un, too. She put in some ginger today."

Excitedly responding, "How nice! I was hoping she would be here, but at least she mixed the tea."

"Here you are ma'am. Everything ready," Winnie smiled, "I'll carry it for you."

"Thank you, Winnie." I added as I followed her to the parlor. It never failed; Astra was never around to meet our clients. She was off gallivanting with "meetings," which meant pleasantries for rendezvous with one of her many beaus. I reminded her all the time to be careful because the wrong person seeing her out unchaperoned would ruin her reputation. She always threw caution to the wind. On one hand, I admired her forwardness, but on the other, I loathed the way she disrespected our father. If Astra would only follow the politeness of society, she could find a husband and settle down. She already had one beautiful quality about her: her tea recipes.

Astra could mix the most flavorful teas with flowers and herbs from our garden. Unfortunately, she would rather be caught dead than be outside tending to the garden, but she would happily take the fruits of my labor to create delightful tea concoctions. I guess it was a wonderful trade after all–I tended the garden, and she mixed the teas. What more could two sisters want?

Upon entry into the parlor, my father and Mrs. Richardson were talking when Winnie and I arrived with tea and scones. "Mrs. Richardson, I hope you enjoy the tea. My sister mixes different dried flowers, herbs, and spices with black tea leaves to create several variations for us. Winnie just told me Astra added ginger to this one."

Mrs. Richardson responded with a simple smile, "How delightful."

"I apologize for her absence, but she had an engagement to attend to."

"Dear girl, thank you," she said as Winnie handed her a cup and a saucer, "Hopefully, I will get to meet her to thank her for this ginger tea. It is quite scrumptious."

"Asphodel, we have finalized everything Mrs. Richardson wants. She is extremely organized and brought a thorough list. I will discuss the list with you later today so we can make all the necessary arrangements." Mr. Willoughby instructed.

"Yes, Papa."

Before Papa could say anything else, Mrs. Richardson, looking at me shyly, politely interjected, "Mr. Willoughby, may I speak to you in private?"

"Yes, ma'am. Asphodel, that will be all for now. Thank you."

"Mrs. Richardson, it was a pleasure to meet you. Again, my condolences. We will take care of all your needs. Goodbye, for now." I responded.

Mrs. Richardson bowed her head as I walked out of the parlor and shut the door for them to talk privately. If she was so thorough to make a list, I wonder why she was so secretive now. Maybe Papa will share what she said with me later. Or will he?

Chapter 3

I decided not to pry into the conversation Papa had with Mrs. Richardson. If he wanted to tell me what they discussed, he would do it later. After lunch, I decided to go outside and tend to the garden. The weather was lovely with an overcast sky of billowing, fluffy clouds acting as an umbrella from the sun, providing protection to us patrons of nature. There was a soft breeze in the air keeping the temperature down leaving the work to be done in perfect conditions for me.

I put my smock on to keep my dress from getting dirty while I went to weed the herb garden. I loved to garden, but weeds were the worst! If I didn't tend to them every single day, they would take over like a vengeful militia. Spending time in the garden also allowed me to just stop and think about anything I wanted to or anything that came to my mind. Many days I thought of books I had read, flowers, plants, and better ways to help my father with funerary practices. This time also allowed me to think of my father and Astra, worrying over both of them and their futures. I also thought of my mother. I knew so very little about her except for the things my father and Cousin Lucy told me. I always wondered if she would be proud of me as I enjoyed helping my father. If she were here, would my life be different from where I would be out in society like Astra? Who knows, and it does not even matter because these were the cards I was dealt with the day I was born. I am better than playing "oh, woe is me."

About that time, a voice called out to me, "Asphodel!" It was Astra back from whatever adventure she devised today. "I'm back and what a lunch I had. Alfred drove me in his carriage to our neighboring town to a very expensive restaurant just to have split-pea soup. Can you believe it?"

"I CAN believe you would do something like that!"

"That is not the point I am trying to make dear sister! Split-pea soup! He did not even ask me if I liked split-pea soup, let alone peas before we arrived. He just told me to meet him next to the florist where he gave me this nosegay and then proceeded to tell me to get in his carriage because we were going to lunch without a word as to where. When we arrived, I thanked him for bringing me to this lavish establishment as we were seated. He told me not to bother with the menu because he had already told the waiter what to bring. So, if you could have seen my face when they brought out the split-pea soup and Alfred said to me, 'Darling, split-pea soup is what they are known for here. I could not wait to share this with you.' I was mortified and had to tell him how much I hated peas. I think I truly hurt his feelings."

"Oh, Astra, I am sure he will get over it, and he will be basking at your feet once again tomorrow." I giggled.

"Tomorrow I will go and see Christopher, but Alfred I am sure will be calling on me again by the end of the week," Astra sighed.

Just as I was about to tell Astra about our latest client, Winnie stepped outside to remind us to go and clean up for supper. I had not realized how long I had stayed out in the garden. I gathered my tools to place them in the shed and then I gathered my basket with all of my herb harvests. Astra waited for me to see what I had collected, "What herbs were plentiful today?"

"I have lots of mint and rosemary. I almost forgot, I also clipped some lemon balm."

Astra replied, "Lemon balm is so nice. I think I might try mixing it with the rosemary for something different. We will see."

We walked into the house together and I gave my basket to Winnie. We went upstairs to get ready for dinner as we parted at the top of the stairs to go to our adjacent rooms. About an hour later, dinner would be served. This gave me time to take a bath, wash up from my stint in the garden, and change into a fresh dress suitable for our everyday occasion. Since I knew we were not having company, and tonight would be just like any usual evening as a family, I put on a light-blueish gray frock made of cool cotton because I felt so warm after being outside most of the afternoon. I wanted something that would breathe on my skin.

Fifty minutes later, I was descending the stairs heading into the dining room. I made it to the dinner table before my sister. Even though we did not invite guests, she always had to make an entrance. My father was there waiting for Astra and me. "Asphodel, you look lovely. It is so nice to see you put on something with a little color. Just because you are my right-hand assistant, does not mean you must wear dark and dreary colors all the time. Why don't you go shopping with Astra some afternoon and pick you out a frock made out of a pale green or pink hue? My dear, I do worry about you being around so much death."

"Papa, do not worry about me. I enjoy working with you and helping you with our clients. I was happy to take over from Cousin Lucy. Anyways, I do dislike shopping with Astra because it always turns into shopping for her rather than her helping me pick something for myself. If I do decide to buy a dress, I will do it alone." I responded intently.

Just as I was finishing my last statement right on cue and ten minutes late, Astra arrived in a bright turquoise cotton dress with a high collar fitted to her just so with her hair half up and down and her ringlets bobbing to her brilliant personality. "Asphodel, you should let me take you shopping. You would not know how to properly choose a dress and would need me." Astra insisted.

"You did not need to eavesdrop. No, I want to shop by myself. If I need help, I will rely on the ladies in the shop. However, I do not need a new dress, so this topic needs to end, please."

We sat down to a usual dinner. Winnie began serving our first course, which was a vegetable soup. None of us spoke to each other for a while until our main course was brought in. We were served pork cutlets with carrots and peas. "Winnie, why do we have to eat peas with every meal?" Astra barked.

"Astra, peas are in season, so we eat what comes out of the garden. Please mind your manners, child." Mr. Willoughby commanded.

"Yes sir, but…" Astra replied before being cut off by Papa.

"I told you to mind your manners. I have enough on my mind and then you start ranting about peas for goodness' sake. Be grateful Astra!"

Winnie was an amazing cook. After we finished our meal, Winnie surprised us with a dessert, which was not a common addition for most meals. We only normally had dessert when we hosted a dinner for friends. "Winnie, this is such a nice surprise. What is it?" Mr. Willoughby asked.

Blushing, Winnie responded, "Oh sir, I do hope you all like this. I wanted to try something different. It is a cold soup made of pear, honey, and some spices. I thought once the summer really sets in when it is blazin' hot, this might be a nice refreshin' dish."

We all tried it as she patiently waited. I thought her eyes would pop out of her head with anticipation. "Winnie, this is delightful!" I complimented her.

"Yes, I do agree with Asphodel. This is a quite clever recipe," Astra added and then mumbling under her breath, "so much better than pea soup."

Mr. Willoughby, rolling his eyes at Astra, satisfyingly said, "Winnie, you have out done yourself. Not only giving us a treat, but coming up with such an original dessert. Thank you."

"Thank you so much. I am so happy you all like it. I won't overdue its welcome by making it all the time, but I will be makin' this again." Winnie left for the kitchen beaming with pride.

"Papa, do you have a plan for getting started on Mr. Richardson for tomorrow?" I asked.

"Yes, Asphodel, I do. Let us plan on starting at seven in the morning so we can get everything ready. Mrs. Richardson was adamant about us being punctual."

"She seems like a very nice lady. Did she say much about her husband or family?"

"She told me she was taken in by another branch of the Richardson family when she was a young woman. They made her a ward because their only child, a son, had died. They met her based on the son's situation and felt bad for her and took her in. She didn't go into why they felt bad for her, just that they did. She said that once she started attending family gatherings and balls, she met Guy Richardson, a cousin to the family who took her in. They courted for a short time and were married. They had one son. She gave very basic details about herself. I'm guessing because she is still in shock at losing her husband. Her son has been away at school, but will be here before the funeral. Apparently, he has finished his schooling and plans to move back here to help take care of her."

"I am glad she will have someone to look after her. I really like her…" I added.

Astra interrupted, "Papa, tomorrow…"

"Do not 'Papa, tomorrow' me young lady. I was just about to tell you I need you home tomorrow."

"Why? You do not need me for the funeral details. You have Asphodel!"

"I need you for something else," he replied.

"What?"

"We will speak about this in my office after dinner and not before. Understand?"

Papa seemed preoccupied as if something was on his mind. "Papa, are you feeling alright?" I interrupted.

"Oh yes. I just need to speak with Astra, and I was waiting until we were all finished to mention it."

"I can leave if you need me to; I'm finished with my soup."

Mr. Willoughby answered, "Thank you dear, this is just something Astra and I need to discuss by ourselves."

"Asphodel can stay. I do not care if she hears whatever it is you want me to do. Why can't we just talk in here?" Astra asked demandingly with a curt tone.

"I guess this is as good a place as any. I know sometimes the walls have ears, but I guess that is every room. Astra, I need you to be willing to listen to what I have to say with an open mind."

"Yes, Papa." Astra defeatedly answered as she looked up from her soup with inquisitive eyes peering at my father. I could tell she was furious. Her green eyes brightened to the color of the dinner peas she hated so much.

As I left the dining room, I closed the doors, giving them privacy. With Papa excusing me from the conversation, I wondered if he found out about Astra's dallying with her beaus unaccompanied. I walked up the stairs slowly, so curious and hoping Astra would fill me in later. Truly, whatever it was, it was none of my business if it was not something that affected me. Time would tell.

I reached my room and decided to prepare for bed early. I put on my dressing gown and robe and sat down to read. I had not started a book in a while because we had been so busy lately, and I did want to begin reading the book, *The Woman in White*, by Wilkie Collins, I picked up a few weeks ago.

I felt like I had read for hours when I looked at the clock and it had only been thirty minutes. Astra had not come up the stairs yet. It made me wonder how serious their conversation was getting. I kept reading. About fifteen minutes later, I heard shouting coming from the dining room, then a door slam. It seemed as if my father was chasing Astra to stop and continue talking with him. "Astra, you come back here at once! You will listen and you will do as I say!"

"I WILL not! I will do with my life as I please and you cannot have me do what you are asking. It is not fair!" Astra yelled as she hurriedly ran up the stairs stomping as she went. I could hear her turn quickly towards her room with no hesitation as I heard an extremely loud slamming of her door. This gave me pause, what did Papa want her to do? Should I go check on him or just leave it be. I crept surreptitiously to my bedroom door and peeked outside. I could just see Papa standing at the bottom of the stairs, one hand on the railing and one hand over his eyes, shaking his head. A whimper wafted out of his mouth as I heard him utter softly, "Belladonna, what am I to do? I wish you were here to help me."

On hearing his woeful words, I carefully shut my door without a creak as I saw Papa ascend the stairs disheveled and defeated.

Chapter 4

The next morning, I arose early as Papa suggested, going into the kitchen for breakfast before my workday began. I had lots to do to get ready for the Richardson funeral. I found Winnie pittling around, but no Papa or Astra. "Good morning, am I up earlier than everyone except you?"

"Oh no, your father is in his office and Astra hasn't come down yet. Mr. Willoughby instructed me to just leave her be. He said if I disturb her, she might bite my head off."

"I see." I drank a quick cup of coffee and had a piece of toast and a piece of bacon before I scurried into Papa's office to ask what I needed to do first.

"Good morning, Papa. Did you sleep well?"

"Um, not so good, but I'll be fine. Why don't you have a seat, and we will get to working on the Richardson funeral. You know, Mrs. Richardson wants the wake here in our parlor."

"Oh, no, you two discussed most of the details without me because she gave you such an organized list. We have not had a wake in a few months. I will make sure the parlor is spotless. Does she need any mourning attire or accouterments?"

"No, she is well prepared in that area. If you could work on the parlor and the invitations. Oh, let me see, here is the list." He handed it to her after sorting through some papers on his desk, "and she wants memorial cards. Here is the information she wants printed on those. Any questions?"

"Yes, when will the wake be?"

"We will open the house next Monday around 1:00 pm and allow mourners to visit until 8:00 pm that evening. She wants to make sure those who are travelling will have time to stop by before the funeral the next day. Anything else?"

"Not about the Richardsons, but since you asked if I had any other questions."

He stopped her before she could even begin, "Asphodel, please do not ask me about what Astra and I discussed last night. You will find out all in due time."

I interjected, "But Papa, I was just going to ask if you were okay. I was not going to be nosy about your conversation."

"Oh, Asphodel, you are too kind to me. I wish your sister was more like you. I am doing okay, but what I have asked Astra to do will ensure my legacy lives on for another generation. I must not speak about it now because a few things need to happen first. Please be patient with me, and especially Astra. Leave her be today. I would even stay away from her and just let her do what she wants. She will come around."

"Yes sir. I am going to work on these items. Let me know if you need me to do anything else." I wanted to say more, but I did not want to seem as if I was wanting to gossip, so I just walked out of the room. I went to get my hat and reticule so I could go to the printers. I spoke with Winnie and told her I would return shortly. She intimated Astra was still in her room.

The printer was only about seven blocks away and it was a delightful morning for a walk into the more urban part of the city. We were just on the outskirts of town and so I observed beautiful trees and flowers along my short little trip. The one place I loved to take a detour in was Paradise Park. There was a mystical lake with a fountain, a little bridge to cross it, a gazebo, and so many Willow Oaks, Red Maples, Sweetgums, and Dogwoods encasing the entire park. The flowers and plants were abundant: Coneflowers, Milkweed, Iris, Foxglove, and so many types of ferns. Walking through this heavenly place reminded me of the poem, "To One in Paradise," by Edgar Allan Poe:

I wish all these flowers were mine; however, I was just happy to walk through this exquisite place. And, after all, I had my asphodels at home.

Taking my little detour only added about ten minutes and I arrived at the printer at nine o'clock. I must have been their first customer because they had not even turned the closed sign to open from the window. Even with this, the door was open.

"Miss Willoughby, it is nice to see you. What brings you in today?" Mr. Meredith, the owner of the print shop, asked me.

"Good morning, I need to place an order for invitations and memorial cards for the Richardson funeral."

"Oh yes, I heard about the gentleman passing. I don't believe I ever met the family, but I haven't heard anything bad about them, so they must be good people. I think they only lived here for about ten or so years."

I responded, "Yes sir, I think that is right. Mrs. Richardson is quite a nice lady. She had a list made and had chosen everything before coming to see us. Here is the pattern she wants and what she wants written on both the invitations and the cards."

"Let me see," as he took the notes from me to match up with what he already has in the shop, "she is organized, I have all of these in house. I will have these ready this afternoon. Come by around three o'clock."

"Thank you, that will be perfect. I can mail them this afternoon as well. Thank you again, Mr. Meredith. I will see you then." I smiled, turning to leave.

As I started my journey back home, I strolled along peering in shop windows when I came across the dress shop. In the window was a lovely everyday dress made of a silk fabric in a sage color. It resembled the same shade of my sage in my herb garden. The dress was a polonaise style as the skirt had a ruffle at the bottom with the whole thing in solid color. The jacket had ruffles on the sleeves and edges with a little sage belt for cinching it up. The fabric for the jacket was sage with a gray stripe. The dress not only caught my eye, but intrigued me like many had never before. Maybe Papa was right–I should wear some other colors besides my grays and blacks. I inquired inside about the dress and to find out the cost before thanking the dressmaker and heading back through the park. I would talk to Papa about this tonight, and maybe Astra, too.

Since my errand at the print shop took only a short time, I decided to stop at the gazebo because no one was around. The gazebo overlooked a wildflower garden that was just breathtaking. I pulled my journal out of my reticule to make some notes about the wildflower garden: the types of flowers and colors. Engulfed in my own little flower world, I almost did not hear a voice trying to get my attention.

"Pardon me, do you mind if I sit on the other side of the gazebo?" A gentleman asked.

"I apologize I was so deep into my notes I almost did not hear you. Of course, do not mind me at all."

"Thank you, miss. I am a little early for an appointment. As I was walking toward my destination, I happened upon this park. It is lovely."

I looked up again, smiling, and studying him before I answered since small talk with strangers was not my forte. He was young, but not too young, maybe around thirty. He was fairly complected, had brown hair that seemed to naturally part on the side, and eyes, reminding me of the sea. His height was tall, maybe six feet or a little more. He wore a dark grey suit, and strangely, had a black ribbon attached to his lapel–someone he knew had died recently. I came out of my fog of gazing at him, "Yes, it is quite lovely. Anytime I go to the shops, I always pass through here."

He looked down at his pocket watch and exclaimed, "Oh, the time, I need to be on my way. I am sorry if I interrupted your thoughts. Do have a delightful day!" He stood up and walked toward town, but not before giving me a little wave goodbye.

I decided I had better be on my way home. I did have tasks to do in the parlor as well as in the garden. I scooped up my journal and pencil and began my walk home. As I started, I could not help but think about Astra and what in the world my father had asked her to do. Hopefully, I will find out soon enough.

Chapter 5

I arrived home to find Astra had still not left her room; moreover, Winnie had taken up a breakfast tray upon her request. I did as my father asked and stayed far away from her room. I decided to work on the parlor, not that it was dirty or cluttered, but I wanted to make sure the room was fitting for mourners. Additionally, I needed to move around some furniture to make room for the bier and coffin. I also needed to bring out more chairs. As I was tidying up and heaving furniture, my hair fell and I looked a mess, which did not matter, we did not have any appointments made for today.

About forty-five minutes into my labor, a pleasant knock on the door startled me. I said to myself, "Who in the world was calling? I must be such a frightful mess," as I peered into the hallway mirror. Indeed, I was met with the frightful mess looking back at me. I tried quickly to press my hair back and dust myself off, but it was almost hopeless. "Oh well, this is what they get for calling without an appointment." I moved into the foyer and opened the door to our visitor. To my surprise, it was the gentleman I sort of met at the gazebo, but something about him was different. Ah, he now had a top hat with crepe adorning the brim almost all the way to the top.

"Good morning!" he said as he bowed after removing his hat.

I was mortified at how I looked. I should have asked Winnie to answer the door, but I was impulsive, and moved to greet our visitor too swiftly. "Good morning, I guess it is still morning. Won't you come in. Did you make an appointment?"

"Yes, yes, I did, with a Mr. Willoughby."

"Oh, I had no idea he had made an appointment with someone. Please come in and go right into the parlor here. I will go get him." I showed him to the parlor and immediately went to my father's office.

"Papa, there is a young man waiting to see you in the parlor. Why did you not tell me you made an appointment with a client?"

"Asphodel, this is not a client. I will fill you in after I meet with this young man."

Confused, I responded, "Yes, Papa, but…"

"Go and bring him here. No questions right now, please."

I nodded and went back to the parlor, trying to fix my mussed self back to presentability on the way. "Mr. ah, I am so sorry. I do apologize; I did not gather your name at the door."

"My name is Benjamin Richardson. It is a pleasure to make your acquaintance." He stood up and bowed again with a grand politeness.

"Mr. Richardson, my father will see you now. Please follow me." Still stunned her father would be this mysterious, I was at a loss for words.

"So, you must be Miss Astra Willoughby?"

"Oh, I am not thinking properly today. I should have told you my name. I am not Astra. I am Asphodel."

"Is Astra your sister?" he mused.

"Yes, she is my twin sister," I answered as we reached the door to my father's office, "It is also a pleasure to meet you Mr. Richardson."

He nodded, entering my father's office, as Papa indicated for him to shut the door. This must be Mrs. Richardson's son. I wonder why he did not come with his mother to attend to his father's funeral details. Wait, how did he know about Astra?

Chapter 6

I went back to the parlor to finish working, trying to focus on the Richardson funeral, and not on the conversation between Papa and Benjamin Richardson. Time moved quickly as I finished up, looking at the grandfather's clock to see how late it was: two o'clock. I worked through lunch and now it was almost time to pick up my order from the printer. Hastily, I ran upstairs, seeing Astra's door still shut, to my room to freshen up.

Heading back downstairs, I realized I had a few minutes to eat something before going back to town. I poured a glass of milk and placed some grapes and cheese on a plate, sitting down at the kitchen table. I ate peacefully and hurriedly. I was surprised no one was around; where was everybody? As I finished up, I went by my father's office to tell him I was leaving, when I found the door still closed. I knew my father well; therefore, I turned around to run my errand, leaving him to continue his conversation with the Richardson son.

My journey into town did not take long as I did not stop at Paradise Park to linger and daydream. I just had to pick up the invitations, take them to the post office where I placed them in the envelopes I had already addressed for sending out. I arrived home to the quiet house I left just a little while ago. I placed my reticule and hat in my room before going back downstairs. I decided to go see if Papa was by himself or not. Luckily, I found him alone and working. I gave a shy knock before entering, "Papa, is it okay to come in?"

"Oh yes, come right in dear. I am about finished with some things for the day. How are preparations coming?"

"The printer finished everything by three, so I was able to mail the invitations this afternoon. In between visits to the printer, I prepared the parlor for the wake. Everything is ready."

"Wonderful! Thank you, you know I appreciate everything you do around here." He offered genuinely.

"You are welcome, I love helping you. Papa, may I ask you about what is really going on with you and Astra? I have never seen her so angry and distant by shutting herself up in her room."

"Asphodel, all in good time. There were a few details I had to work out today before I discussed plans with her. After dinner, I will explain everything. Thank you for your patience and for not prying too much. If you would, please ask Astra to come down so I may speak with her."

"I will and thank you, Papa. I just want what is best for our family, whatever it is."

"I hope you feel the same way when you find out."

Chapter 7

I entered the dining room as Astra walked in front of me from the kitchen without excusing herself. "Astra, please do not take out your anger on me. I have not done anything to you."

"Speak for yourself. I don't want to hear it, Asphodel. I am in no mood!" She firmly claimed.

My father came in, seeming to walk on eggshells as he sat down in his usual place. "Good evening, girls." Papa gently said as if not wanting to poke the bear that was Astra as she glared at him as her pupils lit up as shimmery knifepoints.

Winnie brought in a salad made from vegetables from our garden. It was quite nice. She explained she would not be serving soups for a little while as temperatures were starting to rise each day with the summer season swimming in with sweltering heat and humidity. We ate quietly with few words spoken. I do not believe anyone wanted to speak in fear of what might happen. Before Winnie brought out our fruit for dessert, Astra asked to be excused, and my father granted her wish quickly. She disappeared from the table as if she was a shadow in the wind. I looked up at Papa and gave him a slight grin to let him know everything would be okay.

"Asphodel, I need to make you aware of some changes that will be going on around here. All these things will begin after the Richardson funeral. You remember the day Mrs. Richardson was here to make her husband's arrangements?" He asked.

"Yes sir, she was so organized, more than anyone I had ever seen before."

"Yes, there was a reason for her orderliness. Her son, Benjamin, whom you escorted to my office today, just finished school. He finished his medical program at the University of Virginia in May and has been working with a local undertaker in Charlottesville. He wants to become a full-time undertaker. Mrs. Richardson and her husband supported his decision, as she still does, but she wants him to live closer to her now that her husband has passed on. Since her son has been working with the other undertaker, he guided her on the list to provide us."

"I see, so is he going to apprentice with you?" I asked hesitantly.

"Yes, sort of, at least at first." He added.

"What do you mean at first?"

"After the Richardson funeral, Benjamin will begin working with me as an apprentice to learn more about undertaking and to learn the way of our family business. Now, I want you to know that I still need you, too. This does not mean I don't want you doing all the tasks you are already doing."

"Thank you Papa for stating that. I was about to ask. So, why is Astra so mad? Why is she so mad at you over this? She is not part of the family business, so it should not affect her."

"Well, child, some things are going to affect her. When Mrs. Richardson spoke to me about her son. I was very open to him coming to work for, or with, me. I am not getting any younger, and I do need help with preparing the bodies. She had heard I have been a widow for eighteen years with two daughters, so she came up with an idea. This next part is what she wanted to say to me in private."

As he said this, I felt a lump in my throat wondering what was coming next. I felt like this was not going to infringe on me, but I began to feel anxious and nauseated at the anticipation.

"Asphodel, she wanted to propose that we arrange for Benjamin to marry one of my daughters. She suggested the idea to her son, and he was not opposed, but wanted to meet and speak with me first before he decided. His visit this afternoon answered all those decisions. After he and I had that talk, I thought long and hard on who would be the better match for this young man, even before I met him. You know the business, and so I thought about how you and he could marry and run the business so I could retire. However, I thought about how social Astra is and how she could learn the business." Papa explained.

My head was spinning at the thought of this for myself, or even Astra. Would Papa really do this to one of us? "Is this why Astra is so angry at you?"

"Yes, but there is another larger reason why she is mad, not just at me, but at you. Let's be honest, even though we should not speak of this, Astra does not follow proper etiquette when it comes to her beaus. I am not fooled! I also know you know about her escapades. I know she gallivants around with them to restaurants and the theater unchaperoned. I'm sure the busy bodies in town gossip about her actions and how I have not tamed that child. Marrying her to a gentleman from a respectable family would calm her down and build up her reputation; let alone, provide more respect for our family."

"So, why is she mad at me?"

"Because she is the one I have chosen to court properly and marry Benjamin Richardson. When I spoke to her initially, she could not fathom that I would ask her to number one, arrange a marriage for her; and number two, ask her to learn the side of the business that you do. She feels since you already know the business and you have no possible suitors, you should be the one to be married off."

"You said I could keep doing my own work for you?" I said, raising my voice, feeling a tear coming to my eye.

"Yes, yes, the only matter that will change for you is teaching Astra about the business. Once she is educated, she can help you, so the burden is not all on you. Please do not get upset, Asphodel. I have enough dealing with your sister."

"Oh Papa, I do not know how you are going to pull this off with Astra coming around, but I will help you." I offered.

He finally smiled the first time during this whole conversation, "Thank you, I think if we work on her together, she will be okay with this. You met young Mr. Richardson. He is quite handsome and debonair. He is charming and quite intelligent. Once she meets him, and sees for herself, she will come to like this idea."

"I hope you are right." I said as I thought about how free-spirited Astra actually is. She has been like this since I can remember. Her independence *had been always excessive and habitual.* Could she change? Would she change for Papa? Or herself?

Chapter 8

After my conversation with Papa, I was restless thinking about this situation with the Richardsons, so I went for a walk since it was not quite dusky yet. It started to get a tad bit dark, but there was a full moon, so its light illuminated my path. As I was walking down the center path in the cemetery to my favorite bench, I heard something, but I could not make out what it was. I stopped only using my acute hearing to listen, not moving an inch. I figured it was a rabbit or squirrel, but then, I heard what seemed like words. I quietly looked around, but saw nothing, the moonlight my only form of light shining on the asphodels like little torches glowing on the green grass. "Who is there?" I hesitantly whispered.

No one replied, and so I waited, feeling like a statue who cannot move from being anchored to the ground. The air seemed thick with a hushed haze giving reflections from the moon like a mirror. I questioned my safety, even though I never felt unsafe here before. I slowly turned to look at the house, thinking maybe someone called me to come back, but there was no one. Becoming a little skittish, I felt frozen to turn back around, but I quaveringly moved my right foot softly… "Asphodel…" An eerie voice called out, but I saw nothing.

"I cannot see you. Please tell me who you are?" I asked, louder now.

No sounds uttered from any being. I now felt frightened, but I was not sure if I could turn to run to the house. As I was nurturing my gumption, I saw a figure move between two trees and then behind a tombstone. I was stifled in silence because I did not know who it was. I remained still and watched. A few minutes went by, and the figure was clear again. It was like he or she stood up from bending down by the tombstone. I could tell now it was a woman. I watched her as she stared at the tombstone before walking toward the front gate. As clearly as I could see her, she walked closer and closer to the gate. She had her hand on the latch and then did something mysterious. She turned to me, nodded at me, and then vanished!

I put my hands on my eyes as I rubbed them to feel as though I was seeing things more clearly. My eyes must be playing tricks on me. We must have left the gate unlocked and someone must have been visiting a loved one's grave. Suddenly, I heard my name said with glee right next to me. Should I open my eyes or just run? Again, I heard my name, "Asphodel!"

I turned to my right, and saw a girl. A girl I actually knew, my friend Berenice sitting next to me on my bench. Berenice was about the same age as me and she was *to the beauty of fair Greece*. She wore her golden ringlets a little different from how I styled my own hair. She said she did not like the more modern styles, so he wore them hanging on each side of her head. I think she loved Greek mythology and wanted to feel like a goddess. She had spirited eyes giving over to her overflowing attitude about life and living it.

"Did I startle you?" she asked.

"A little, yes. You see…" I hesitated as she was looking intently at me to finish, but I did not want to seem like I was crazy mentioning I saw a spirit, so I changed the subject, "Oh, never mind, how are you?"

"I am so well! I have been in the meadow behind my home dancing gracefully among the wildflowers. I was practicing the Quadrille."

"The Quadrille! Oh, Berenice, how? It takes a partner and three other couples, silly girl."

"Even practicing by myself, I can still pretend I have a partner and just do my part of the steps."

I laughingly responded, "I guess so. I am so happy you stopped by, even though it is so late. You have cheered me up. Astra is mad at me, again, and now she loathes Papa. He is going to make her learn the business, and marry someone she has not even met yet."

"Oh Asphodel, I can imagine she might never get over this. Will she go through with it?"

"I don't know. Time will tell I guess. Why are you out so late?" I wondered.

"I had to run an errand. I took a book my cousin borrowed from one of his friends and returned it for him. Your house was on the way back, so I thought I would stop by for a little while."

"Okay, you should be careful out this late."

"I'll be fine. I probably should go, though. I do not want anyone worrying about me."

I waved as she stood up from the bench to leave, "I hope to see you soon. Please send a note to let me know when you can come by again."

"I will. Keep your chin up. I have a feeling everything will turn out just fine for your family in due time." Berenice said as she started walking away.

"What are you, a fortune teller?" I said humorously.

"No, just one who has a certain intuition for these things. Goodnight."

I watched her walk through the tombstones up to the gate. She turned around, waved, and vanished just like the other woman. I had not paid attention before. I guess at night from where I am sitting, it makes people look ethereal as they are leaving. After all, the humidity was high, and it did make the air seem as though a thick haze hosted the moisture like a London fog.

Chapter 9

Monday morning came quickly as the past few days hardly any of us spoke to one another. Papa and I had everything ready for the wake. We only had a few small tasks to complete before one o'clock when the mourners would arrive. Papa decided to keep Astra out of all these arrangements with the Richardsons because Mrs. Richardson and Benjamin would not be themselves during these next sorrowful days. He even told Astra to go stay with Cousin Lucy until Wednesday. When he made this suggestion, I saw the wheels in Astra's mind on high gear at what she might plan being away from home. Cousin Lucy spoiled us, so she would not tell Astra no to anything. Oh, praise be to God, I hope she would not do something outrageous and ruinous to rebel against Papa. She was grown, so these were her mistakes to make.

One o'clock arrived and the family was set up in a reception line in the foyer to receive the visitors. It seemed the entire town attended with how many people came and went throughout the day. I felt so bad for Mrs. Richardson having to stand there all this time. She needed her own time to grieve; however, societal norms required this to be proper. When fewer people were entering, I checked on the matriarch, and she always indicated she was holding up very well. Young Mr. Richardson continued to eye me every time I did this. I wondered if he thought I was Astra.

The final hour arrived, and Mrs. Richardson went to sit down because hardly any visitors or mourners stopped in. I went into the parlor and brought her some tea. "Thank you, my dear. It is Asphodel, isn't it?" she asked timidly so not to make a mistake.

"Yes ma'am. Is there anything else you need?"

"No, thank you, my dear. Will Astra come down before we leave?"

45

"No ma'am, she is staying with my cousin Lucy for a few days. She never, uh rarely, helps Papa with wakes and funerals." I thought I better start saying rarely instead of never helping build her up a little bit.

"I see. Well, thank you, my dear, for everything you and your father have done for our family. You both have made this an extremely easy process for myself and my son. You have met him, haven't you?" she asked.

"Oh yes, one day last week," hearing a noise and looking at the door, "I see a man and woman coming in to see you. I will excuse myself and check with you in a little while." I felt as if I sprinted out of the parlor into the hallway because just as those people were coming in, Benjamin was walking towards me. I decided to pause there for a moment, breathing heavy, as if I was caught with my hand in the cookie jar after bedtime. I patted my forehead, making sure I was not perspiring. I do not know why I was acting like this. I was being an immature schoolgirl. As I was pressing my hand to my hair to check a hair pin, I felt another presence beside me unexpectedly.

As I turned to look with my hands in my hair, I discovered Benjamin was staring at me with a wry smile. "Good evening, Miss Willoughby. I came out to thank you for being so kind to Mother and me. Are you digging for gold in your hair?" He asked sarcastically.

I was mortified by him finding me like this, even though I should not care, but for some reason, I did. "That's funny, Mr. Richardson! I felt my hair falling and was hunting for my pin if you must know." I responded with a slight bit of facetiousness of my own.

"I wanted to ask you something. I thought I heard you say the other Miss Willoughby, your sister, was away for a few days. Is that right?"

"Yes, Papa felt as if she should be away from your father's funeral proceedings before she is introduced to you. She will return most likely on Wednesday, but I do believe my father and your mother are going to arrange a meeting for the two of you. May I ask you something?"

"Of course, ask and I shall answer."

"When will you begin your apprenticeship with my father?"

"Next Monday. Mr. Willoughby wanted me to have a few more days with Mother to wrap up some details and to just have more time to grieve. Your father is an incredible man."

"I do agree, and I do like that we have that in common." Why did I say something like that? I must be exhausted from all the fuss of today. "If you will excuse me, Mr. Richardson, I need to tend to something in the kitchen." I nodded with a little bow and turned quickly before he could stop me for more conversation.

I meandered in the kitchen until all the guests had left about eight thirty. Papa retrieved me to the parlor to say goodnight to the Richardsons. We said our pleasantries and they left after reassuring everything would be ready for the funeral in the morning. "Papa, I am so tired. Is there anything I need to do before I go up to bed?"

"No, we are extremely prepared for the morning. You go on up. I have a few small things to attend to before I retire, but nothing involves you. Goodnight, my dear."

"Thank you Papa, and goodnight." I replied quietly as I walked towards the stairs to go up to my bedroom. My feet felt like I had on concrete boots. As soon as I entered my room and changed, my head fell on my pillow like a brick. I closed my heavy eyelids and assumed I would fall asleep as speedily as a buzzing fly. However, I found myself thinking about Benjamin. He seemed nice, had a great sense of humor, and he was handsome. "Asphodel, stop thinking this way. I do not even know him, and he is semi-betrothed to Astra." I whispered aloud, pinching myself for thinking such thoughts. I closed my eyelids again, now thinking to myself: What would Astra actually think of him?

Chapter 10

The next day, the funeral came and went without any issues. Mrs. Richardson thanked us again for handling everything impeccably. She was a stoic woman; however, it was quite obvious how much she endearingly loved her husband. Benjamin took his mother home rather quickly after the services. Papa and I walked inside the house and settled in the parlor, as we were also exhausted. "Papa, I am going to the kitchen and make us up some tea. I think we could use some."

"Asphodel, I rather like that idea. Do not go to too much trouble."

"Yes, sir." I humored my father as I walked into the kitchen. Winnie actually left the tea kettle out so all I had to do was find one of Astra's concoctions. I set everything up and waited for the water to boil.

Once I heard the piercing whistle, I poured the water into the pitcher before carrying the tray into the parlor. Papa seemed to have nodded off while I was in the kitchen. He works so hard, I really did not want to wake him up. I set the tea service down and began to pour out my tea. The scent of lemon must have wafted into his olfactory senses because all of a sudden, he woke up.

"Oh, Asphodel, did I fall asleep?" He said loudly as he jumped as if he was startled.

"Yes, Papa, you did. I was not going to wake you, but since you are up, I'll pour your tea." As I prepared his tea how he liked it, he decided to become very chatty.

"Asphodel, what do you think of young Mr. Richardson?"

I was quite taken aback by his question. I fibbed just a teeny bit because I had thought about him. "Uh, Papa, I have not really thought about him. He seems quite a nice young man," I hoped I did not come across as disingenuous, "How do you feel about him?"

"I do believe he is going to work out well as my apprentice. I am worried more about him working out for Astra. Actually, Astra working out for him." He said as he gave a little chuckle.

Just as I was about to comment about Astra, she burst into the parlor with a companion walking behind her. "Papa and Asphodel, aren't we the typical two tasting tea together. You two should find something more exciting to do with your time."

"Astra, we just finished with the Richardson funeral. Have some respect for the dead! Would you have us dance a jig as tired as we are? I thought you wouldn't be home until tomorrow. Cousin Lucy, what brings you here?" Papa responded.

"Thomas, I brought Astra back myself. She insisted on going out today and I told her a lady should never go out into town every single day—people will talk. So, I said, if she wanted to go out, it would be home. Besides, I have not been for a visit to see you and Asphodel in a few months. I thought I was due."

"Astra, please sit down with us. Asphodel, would you please go to the kitchen and prepare more tea?" Papa insisted to both of us.

"Yes, Papa." I went to the kitchen, but I could hear most of their conversation because Astra raised her voice, causing Papa to raise his voice even louder. He was scolding her about her escapades and taking advantage of Cousin Lucy. This made me want to go up to my room to stay for the evening. Once more, water boiled; I carried the tray back into the parlor.

As soon as I stepped in, the bickering continued like a repeated chorus out of tune. I sat closer to Cousin Lucy preparing her tea. "Here you are Cousin Lucy," she said as she accepted the cup and saucer made of fine bone china with tiny, delicate dark red roses painted on it.

"Thank you dear, I am so sorry to bring this melodrama home earlier than expected, as you and Thomas are spent, but Astra must begin acting accordingly if she will be accepted by the Richardson boy as his wife." Cousin Lucy explained.

"Oh, it is quite all right. I expect this from her. It has become quite a habit."

They finally had nothing left to say to one another, and so the room became quiet as quiet as if I had just walked down to the basement where Papa prepares the bodies for their funerals. "Well, I made arrangements for us to go to the Richardson's on the following Friday evening for a dinner for you, Astra, and Young Mr. Richardson to be properly introduced. Mrs. Richardson and I felt we should have the dinner at her home since she is in full mourning to keep with proper etiquette, even though this is an unusual circumstance with her mourning rituals. Young Mr. Richardson will begin working here on Monday morning. Are there any questions?"

"No sir," I said agreeingly.

"May I have a new dress for this dinner? I feel I should get something I want if you are going to sell me off." Astra fumed.

"What the Dickens, Astra? How dare you speak of me treating you like property! Arranged marriages are nothing new. I am trying to save your reputation. I understand you are not getting a choice in the matter, but once you meet this young man, I believe you will feel differently. As to a new dress, I would be happy to see you take Asphodel and you both purchase new dresses." Papa exclaimed, feeling hurt and insulted by Astra.

"Papa, Asphodel and I will go to the dressmaker's tomorrow. Thank you." She responded with indignance with a touch of regret.

"Thank you Papa, I actually did see a lovely dress in the window when I went to the printer's the other day. It was in a gorgeous shade of sage green." I added.

"Fine, I am so happy to hear that Asphodel. Now, you girls go to your rooms or find something else to do while I speak to Cousin Lucy."

We curtsied to both of them as we walked out of the parlor, closing the door gently behind us. At the top of the stairs, Astra stopped me from going into my room as I was going to retrieve a book to read outside on the veranda. "Asphodel, be ready in the morning at ten o'clock or I will leave you and go by myself." She said as she quickly stormed into her room like a straight-lined tornado before slamming her door shut.

Chapter 11

Ten o'clock seemed so late, but Astra was not an early bird like me. We walked into town with few words to each other. I felt as though she was still angry with me, but more so at Papa. I decided not to anger her further, so I only spoke to her when she brought anything up to me first.

Even though the dressmaker was not too far from us, it seemed as if we *Had journeyed long, Singing a song, In search of Eldorado.* We paused just outside the door as Astra peered in the windows to see what Madame White had on display. As soon as we entered, the owner came straight up to Astra. "Darling Miss Willoughby, it has been quite too long since we have prepared a dress for you. It is a pleasure to see you again. How may I help you today?"

"Madame, indeed, I have stayed away too long. My sister and I need new dresses to attend a dinner a week from this Friday. We will need two dresses you have on hand rather than custom made. Asphodel told me about the sage green dress in the window and so we know we want that one, but what else do you have for me, maybe in a darker color." Astra suggested.

"Let me think, I do have a navy-blue polonaise style. Would you like to try it on?" Madame White inquired.

"Yes, I would love that."

Madame White took Astra into another room for her to try on the navy dress. She came out beaming, saying it was so beautiful. Indeed, it was; the dress was a polonaise, but very different from the sage green one. It was solid in color and lacked the ruffles my favorite dress was adorned with on the sleeves and on the skirt. The dress was beautiful, but it unfortunately was not as striking as my favorite.

"Asphodel, how do you like it?"

"It is stunning and suits you well."

Astra asked, "Would you wear something like this?"

"Yes, I would."

Madame White interjected, "Asphodel, how about we have you try on the sage green dress."

"Yes ma'am." I beamed as she took me to the other room.

As I sauntered out into the main room, Astra was waiting for me. Her eyes glowed when she saw me. "Asphodel, I have never seen you look lovelier! I knew when I saw that dress in the window it was meant for a very special lady."

"Thank you sister!" I looked at myself in the mirror for a just a few minutes more grinning from ear to ear. As I saw myself, Benjamin entered my mind. Oh, I just must be excited for Astra.

Astra worked everything out with Madame White after measurements were taken to ensure proper fit and the appropriate length for both dresses. Madame White giggled as she took Astra's and my measurements, "You two are exactly alike even to your exact measurements. I should have just measured one of you."

As we left the shop, I felt as though I was walking on air. Madame White explained to us she would have the dresses delivered on Friday morning, the day of the dinner, so she would have enough time to make the necessary alterations. Astra told her she trusted her immensely, and then we were on our way home.

"Asphodel, we were so lucky Madame White had not sold the sage green dress. I think it is one of her finest creations thus far."

"I agree, and I am more excited than I thought I would be."

Astra said before we both were in our own thoughts on the rest of the walk home, "If you wore more pretty things, you would feel like this more often. On Friday next, it will be more than excitement you will feel when you put on your new dress."

Chapter 12

The rest of the week brought no new business since no one in town died. It felt very odd at times realizing our livelihood relied on people who died with sorrowful families needing us to guide them. Papa occupied his time through paperwork, Astra stayed mostly in her room unless she was putting together tea mixtures, and I did my usual reading, gardening, or walking in our cemetery tending to the asphodels around the tombstones.

As the weekend neared, I suddenly remembered Benjamin would start working with us on Monday, and my life would change forever. I would never admit this to Papa, but I was afraid of him not needing me anymore. What would I do? I did not have many friends, just Berenice, and she was never one I could wholeheartedly rely on because I saw her so infrequently. I was also afraid Papa would send me off to live with Cousin Lucy. My place was here among my namesake, the asphodels.

Saturday evening after dinner, Papa retired early to bed so he could be up bright and early to prepare himself and his work area to greet young Mr. Richardson on Monday morning. Astra was in her room, so I decided to read in the parlor. The house was quiet, which made me content so I could focus on my book, *Wuthering Heights*. As I read, I heard a noise in Papa's office, so I stealthily went to investigate. Entering his office, I saw a brief shadow as if a man were present. It quite startled me! I waited a moment before going in to see if I heard anything else. Unfortunately, I did. I heard paper rustling on the desk. I crept on my tip toes as lightly as I could to peer around the door just in case there was a robber. Placing my nervous fingers gently on the sturdy door frame, I cocked my head in a way to stay unnoticed from Papa's desk. What I saw made me freeze with eyes pulsing with blinks so fast I thought I stopped breathing. On his desk, one of the papers was crinkling up, but there was no one in sight. I shivered from head to toe, wondering if I should wake Papa. I decided to wait and see if it stopped or what else might happen.

A few minutes went by with no movement from the paper. Slowly, step by step I inched my way in. I saw nothing but the pieces of the furniture, which belonged there. From the fireplace, I shot myself to Papa's desk chair and sat down furiously, feeling I was fighting for my life. I stared at the rumpled paper for a few minutes so not to disturb what had been made of it. Once I knew it was not going to keep moving, I picked it up, trying to smooth it out on the desk. As I had pressed it out as best as I could, I read its contents. It was the invitation Mrs. Richardson sent Papa for the dinner where Astra would meet Benjamin. This was so odd. Papa must have crumpled this up for some reason and my mind was playing tricks on me with the quietude, the candlelight, and the dark shadows looming from every corner. I was always sensitive to those dark shadows, ever since I was a child. I had an active, creative mind, believing I saw spirits. Papa continued to say they were figments of my imagination, but were they really. At that moment, I heard another noise in the foyer. Oh my! I should have gone to bed when everyone else did.

Leaving the uncrumpled paper on my father's desk in his office, I walked quietly to the foyer. These noises were louder than what I heard earlier. Surely, this must be the workings of a prankster. To my surprise, I did see someone in the foyer moving around. It was Astra! "Dear sister, you just gave me the fright of my life. What are you doing?"

"I thought you had gone to bed. What are YOU doing?" Astra declared.

"I was reading in the parlor, and I heard noises coming from Papa's office, so I went to look…" I stopped talking because she was giving me the look of I do not care, "Oh, never mind. Are you going out?"

"As a matter of fact, yes. I won't be too long. Long enough to be away, but not too long to be back before Papa knows I'm gone. If he does wake up, pretend we never spoke."

"Astra, you promised you would stay home and act like a lady!"

"Shhh, keep it down. You will wake up the dead in the cemetery! I never promised; I just said I would try." She said with a guilty smirk.

"I cannot believe you! You disrespect Papa so much. Just in case something happens, where are you going?" I said, looking on her with disdain.

"As it is none of your business, I am meeting Alfred. His carriage is outside waiting for me."

"What about Christopher? What about Benjamin?" I pried.

"Christopher is not worthy of me. Who is Benjamin?" Astra stated with hate-filled prideful eyes.

As Astra had her back turned opening up the door, I answered her question, "Benjamin is the man you are supposed to marry. You know, young Mr. Richardson."

Astra suddenly stopped, only slightly turning her head, with hate spewing from somewhere beneath the depths of hell. She flew back, "How funny, you are already on first named basis with 'BENJAMIN'? Seems to me you might be a little too familiar yourself."

She eyed me condescendingly after her last comment, and left abruptly. I began to cry. How dare she insult me when she knows I am nothing like her. Running up the stairs, I went to my room and cried myself to sleep.

Around midnight, I heard someone come up the stairs, so I knew she was home. I turned over and attempted to go back to sleep. Restless, I was in stitches as to what to do or if I should tell Papa anything. Should I be selfish and keep this to myself? Or, tell Papa and have Astra making my life miserable for eternity? I guess only time will tell.

Chapter 13

Sunday came and went with all of us keeping to ourselves except when I inquired about the crumpled paper in my father's office. As he was sitting at his desk, I asked if I could talk with him and he acquiesced. "Papa, last night, I heard a strange noise in your office. I went to see what it was, and I found this paper wadded up. I tried to smooth it out as best as I could. I was quite timid and scared entering your office." I explained.

"Oh, Asphodel, houses make strange noises. This house is no stranger to weird and odd things, so stay grounded and you will be fine. I am sure I probably crumbled it up and forgot to throw it away. It is just our dinner invitation to the Richardson's for Friday. It means nothing. I appreciate you telling me and looking out for my papers. You know, paperwork likes to get up and dance sometimes." He said jovially, laughing out loud as I laughed with him.

"I know I am a bit childish sometimes. My imagination runs away with me, especially when I am by myself."

"It is quite all right my dear. I think it is wonderful you have such an imagination. It makes life more enjoyable. Um, on a different note, are you ready to begin working with young Mr. Richardson tomorrow?" He asked a little hesitatingly.

"Of course, why would I be otherwise?"

"Asphodel, I know how you are. You have been helping me for a good while and you like structure. Having him with us will upset our structure somewhat. Mr. Richardson will be a wonderful asset to us, just wait and see."

"Yes, Papa, I know."

Monday morning arrived early. Papa and I ate breakfast it seemed before the rooster crowed, but he wanted us to be ready. We ate with a little haste in order to be finished before Papa's apprentice would make his appearance for his first day. As we were leaving the table, three knocks were heard on the front door. Earnestly, Papa walked speedily to let him in. As he did so, I entered the parlor and sat down. Papa and Mr. Richardson entered the room. "Mr. Richardson, or may I call you Benjamin?"

"Oh yes, Mr. Willoughby. Good morning, Miss Willoughby," he gleefully stated as he bowed and took a seat in a winged back chair next to me.

"Benjamin, I welcome you wholeheartedly to my funerary business. My late wife and I began it many years ago. When she passed, my cousin assisted me, and then when Asphodel was of age, she insisted on helping as my cousin was getting on in age. Asphodel has been such an asset to me. She does an excellent job with all the accoutrements to assist the families. I would actually like you to understand everything about the inner workings of Willoughby Undertakers as you will be joining the family, and eventually running the business."

"Sir, I could not be more humbled to learn from you and to be given this opportunity." Benjamin ecstatically said.

"Good! Well, we should get right to it then. For today, I want you to work with Asphodel and learn the soft side of the business from her. Astra will also be learning this…when the time is right. The Jenson family's grandfather passed yesterday, so they will be coming in to meet with us about arrangements. After we have their choices, you and Asphodel may work together planning everything for them. How does that sound?" Papa asked.

"I am here to learn. I will do whatever you ask me to do. Happily, I know working with Miss Willoughby will provide me the starting point on my apprenticeship. When should I expect to begin working with you?"

"The body of Mr. Jenson will arrive tomorrow. So, your presence is needed then. Any other questions?"

"No sir, thank you again for everything." Benjamin added with sincere pride.

"Young man, your arrival could not be more perfect at this moment." Papa cordially stated as we continued to discuss the Jenson family and what knowledge we knew about them to prepare Mr. Richardson.

Mr. Jenson's son, Robert, arrived right on time for his appointment. He came alone as his wife did not feel it was appropriate to leave the house during her mourning period. Introductions were made briefly, and the discussion of Mr. Wyatt Jenson's wake and funeral were conducted in the same manner. Robert Jenson was a man of no-nonsense when it came to business; moreover, the signs of grief shown in his face and mannerisms as the wrinkles on his face were like new wagon wheel remnants from many travels into town to visit their general store. He portrayed stoicism like no other to appear brave and strong in one of the direst times of his life.

We did not detain him with idle chat. We went straight to the arrangements, allowing him to leave quietly and privately to go back home to grieve with his wife and family. Papa walked him to the door after thank-yous and pleasantries were exchanged between all of us, leaving Mr. Richardson and I alone.

"Miss Willoughby, I am guessing you have ideas about what Mr. Jenson wants. Am I correct in that assumption?"

"Yes, Mr. Richardson, you are quite correct. Once my father comes back in and I check with him on a few things, we may go into the office to start the process." I added without looking up from my notes. I felt him looking at me with his inquisitive eyes, and I just could not look up into those endless pools of blue. I could not get lost in them. If I gazed into them too long, I would drown in utter sorrow. I had Astra to consider.

Papa came back into the parlor as we discussed any questions I had. "Mr. Richardson, please follow me to the office." I invited.

"Asphodel, Benjamin will be working here for a very long time as he will be family in the hopefully, near future. Please drop all these formalities and call this young man Benjamin. Benjamin, please do the same and call my daughter by her first name, Asphodel." Papa insisted.

"Yes, Papa. Benjamin, would you please accompany me to the office?" I gestured toward the hall.

"Why yes, Asphodel. I would be happy to."

We walked the short distance with Benjamin following me as he was now learning our house one step at a time. Arriving in the office, I pulled over a chair to sit by me at my desk so we could work together, and I could show him what I do. I decided to start with the invitations and funeral cards so we could go to the printer before lunch.

"Benjamin, we are going to begin with writing the invitation, and then the funeral cards. Here is one I did…" I stopped as Benjamin interrupted me.

"Asphodel, what a lovely name. Where does it come from?" He asked inquisitively with an element of boyish curiosity and romanticism.

"Uh, Benjamin, pardon me, but we need to get to work. I want to get to the printer before lunch."

"I'm so sorry, I just couldn't help to wonder as we were walking in here." Benjamin apologized.

I decided to give him a short answer so he would focus, "My father named me Asphodel after the flower. It means death. After lunch, I will show you our cemetery where they grow. It will make sense to you why he chose my name when you see them."

"It is one of the most beautiful names I've ever heard. I apologize for being distracted. May I see your previous invitation you were trying to hand me?" He inquired politely as he still continued subtly gazing at me.

I handed him the card as I began to write Mr. Jenson's. After he studied it for a few minutes, he began looking at what I was writing. He did not say a word; he just watched me write. "Asphodel, from seeing this one as to what you are putting down, should you not use this style again. It would be very fitting for this gentleman."

I perused the example invitation I gave him, studying it for several moments as I questioned him about what he was saying, pointing at a specific part when his hand came up to point at the exact spot our fingers touched. I moved away quickly because I was startled almost seeming to feel a spark as our phalanges intertwined. I could see he was embarrassed, but he spoke not a word. "I see what you are meaning. Yes, you are right. I will change it." I offered back as I was so flustered I made a mistake, and he pointed it out to me. Why was I so distracted today?

We continued to work diligently. Benjamin's help actually caused us to finish up much earlier than I could finish the work on my own. I did not fathom this could be completed so quickly. Again, this aggravated me as well. I am very competent; however, his input created more efficiency. Was I jealous or was it something else? I told myself to tamp down these feelings. It was just the first day!

"Benjamin, we are finished and ready to go into town to the printer. I usually just walk because it is not that great of a distance. Let me gather our hats." I hospitably offered.

"Let me. Wait by the front door." Benjamin insisted, walking out of the office to gather our things.

I placed our work in a large envelope and walked to the front door, thinking about the morning. Would he point out my mistakes each day? Or was I just not myself today? At this moment, I did not have the answer; thus, I shan't worry too much about it. Except, my thoughts could not leave this alone. Just as I was engrossed in this conundrum, Benjamin appeared with our hats. He waited for me to place my hat on my head just so, offering his arm to escort me outside. Before taking his arm, I peered into his eyes. As I did, I felt calmed, causing a smile to form on my rose colored lips as he returned a smile as genuine as gemstone pulled right out of a mine. Our gaze was broken as my father walked up behind us to wish us a healthy constitution to the printer. We said our goodbyes to Papa and left the house.

We began our walk with Benjamin insisting he hold the envelope with our work. Heading towards town, we remained silent for a short while. The awkward silence between us caused us both about the same time to ask each other a question interrupting the other. "Ladies first, Miss Asphodel." Benjamin politely declared.

"I was just going to ask what it was like at the university."

He responded, "I enjoyed every minute of it. My entire life was spent learning about classical studies, especially natural philosophies. So, I knew what I wanted to focus on when I arrived just four years ago. I thoroughly loved learning Latin, which became a large part of my studies in biology. I was fascinated with human systems. That led me to want to become an undertaker. Your father is one of the most generous men I have ever met, and I am beholden to him for this apprenticeship."

"University life sounds enchanting with learning so many subjects. My father is very glad you entered our world. He is not getting any younger and you being here gives him lots of options to retire sooner rather than later. He has worked so hard to build the business with respect from the whole town and cities outside Spencerton. How do you like our town?"

"I like it so far. It is quaint and seems just the right size. I know my mother loves it, but with my father's passing, I know if I had moved somewhere else, she would be lost. It was extremely important for me to stay here to watch over her."

I empathetically responded, "I truly understand, only having one parent, creates the children to become guardians to them. I never knew my mother, she died during childbirth."

"I am so sorry. I'm sure she was a splendid lady." He added.

"That is what I have been told and cannot believe otherwise. My father has given Astra and me so much due to her death to make up for her not being here. My mother's midwife, Madame Lucia, stayed on as our governess so we had a mother figure in our lives. She was absolutely a darling of a woman. I would have wanted no other except for my mother, if she could have lived to raise us. Madame Lucia was with us until we were just shy of our eighteenth birthday. She had heart problems and died. I was devastated at the loss. I just assumed Madame Lucia would be with us forever. I loved her like a mother, and she loved Astra, and me like daughters. She is truly missed every day." I spoke mournfully.

Benjamin replied with quiet reserve, "Asphodel, I cannot express to you how sad that makes me feel for you losing your mother and then Madame Lucia. In the little time I have known you, I do believe your mother would be so proud of you and your sister, even though I have not met her. Your woe makes me so appreciative of the time I had with my father, and what I still have with my mother. Thank you for sharing this with me."

"These are things you need to know as you meet Astra later this week. Anything else I can prepare you with I will gladly share."

"Thank you. You are such a considerate lady." He complimented me.

"Oh, you are welcome. I'm just a sister who deeply cares for her twin and what is happening to her. I just want Astra to be happy and settle down." I blushed as I began to speak with such a sweet compliment.

About that time, we arrived at Meredith's Printing House. I introduced Mr. Meredith to Benjamin as Papa's apprentice. They spoke for a bit of time, and then we placed our order. We walked back to the house quietly without as much conversation as before to arrive just in time for lunch.

We ate with Papa while Astra had already left the house for the afternoon. Honestly, it was probably better Astra did stay away during the day this week while Benjamin was starting his apprenticeship. The two of them needed to have the proper introductions awaiting them this coming Friday evening. They were owed every possible appropriate way to start their relationship in the right way. As we arose from the table, Benjamin reminded me of the walk in the cemetery I promised after lunch, and so we went.

"Asphodel, how long has the cemetery been here?" Benjamin asked curiously.

"It has been here longer than the house, dating back to the late sixteen hundreds. The cemetery grew over time, needing a caretaker, so the house was built in 1809. The caretaker just happened to be my grandfather, so the house and the cemetery were passed down to my father." I explained.

"The fields of the cemetery are enchantingly radiant. I have never seen a cemetery more stunning."

We kept walking, getting closer to the tombstones. I guided him to the back, so we could make our way forward to move closer back to the house. Besides, at the back, we had to ascend a hill, so the view was even better. I wanted him to see this for himself.

"These flowers are brilliant, so delicate, almost illuminating the headstones. What are they?" Benjamin asked.

"These are the asphodels. The flowers that guided Persephone between the living world and the world of death. My father looked upon this cemetery after he buried my mother and saw the otherworldly nature of the fields of these forlorn flowers and named me, Asphodel. He realized these were his favorite flowers and the astra was my mother's favorite flower, which my mother named my sister just before she died. I keep all the gardens around the house and also weed through the asphodels to maintain the beauty of the cemetery. We keep it open from dawn to dusk. Many venture in to visit their loved ones, but some enter just to walk in beauty, especially just before dusk, *And where thy footstep gleams* — is an asphodel lighting their path of ethereal moonlight reflecting on each petal." I explained dreamily.

"This cemetery and these flowers seem to mean everything to you. Now, I can see why you protect them so. It is your connection to your mother. It is such a substantially exquisite sentiment to honor her. I will do my best to keep these graves and flowers shielded from harm's way as best as I can. Asphodel, thank you for sharing this with me. Does Astra ever come here to take walks?" Benjamin said with sincere emotion.

"Not really, she only comes out here if she is looking for me. I tend to spend a great deal of time here."

"I see." He uttered almost as a question with an air of mystery.

Chapter 14

Tuesday through Thursday were spent with Benjamin and I picking up the invitations and funeral cards, addressing the invitations, mailing them, and preparing all the other items for the wake, which was taking place the following Monday. Papa left me going through all the arrangements with Benjamin, so he had no questions as to this side of the business. Papa told me he would take over and teach Benjamin his side of the business with the body preparation on the next funeral. For the most part, the week went by teaching him things without any issues; however, we did argue some over the way I did things. I would get very aggravated because he would suggest different ways, but I kept telling him, the way I did things was the way Cousin Lucy before me, and my mother before her always did them, and it all worked swimmingly. I was stubborn, but he was also stubborn. It started me thinking how could he and I work together once Papa was gone.

Then it hit me, Astra would be working with him as his wife after Papa was gone. Where did that leave me? Or would I teach Astra how to make the arrangements, but then she would bail out, leaving me to do everything. She would get away with it because I would always take up for her and she would guilt me into it, still accusing me of killing our mother.

Friday morning arrived with Benjamin and I setting up everything in the parlor for the wake. Elbow to elbow, we were side by side attaching crepe all over the room. He questioned me on why I was adding crepe in certain places. "Benjamin, this is what we do. This covers any of our personal items so the emphasis will be on the Jenson's. It is just what we must do. I cannot believe we are arguing over something this simple. Why must you be so obtuse?"

65

"Asphodel, I am trying to understand all of this. I am not questioning you. I know these are not the things I will be dealing with, but your father wants me to know how to do them. It makes sense because if you are not here…" Benjamin paused as he said those words. He stared at me like he had never before. We had turned to each other, crepe in our hands, eyeing intently into each other's eyes with spellbound intensity. I became nervously elated, unknowing what to do next when Benjamin dropped the crepe from his hands, throwing his arms around me at my waist, planting his tender lips upon mine with an uncontrollable eager passion, unwavering to stop. My arms were trapped inside his embrace, still holding the crepe in my hands. I was taken aback, not knowing what to do, only to follow his lead and give into the savory kiss. Almost at the same time, we broke away from each other, realizing what we had done. The tension had been building all week as we frustrated each other with every turn of each preparation for Mr. Jenson's funeral. The kiss broke the tension like an arrow from Cupid, but realizing the betrayal to Astra was like a lightning bolt from Zeus.

"I am so sorry, Asphodel. I do not know what I was thinking. I am ashamed of myself." Benjamin begging to be forgiven, looking down away from me.

"Please do not apologize. I gave into this as much as you. I am sorry, too. No one has to know what happened. It was nothing, just this one time. You will meet Astra tonight and we will never speak of this again as long as we live." I pleaded.

"Asphodel, again, I am so sorry. Thank you for being so forgiving, but it is not fair to you."

"Astra is your betrothed, the better sister to be your wife. We will work together and become family. No one will ever know this happened. Go home, I will finish all this by myself. The family will see you this evening. You will meet Astra and fall in love with her instantly. I just know it. Now, please go." I insisted, unknowing to him my motivation for him to leave.

"I have no words, Asphodel. You are a wonderful, compassionate woman. I…"

"Please, not another word. Just…go." I implored, holding back guilty tears for the true feelings I had for Benjamin. Sure, I thought he was handsome and philosophical, but I did not know I felt this strongly until he kissed me. Upon family honor, I must do everything in my power to pack these feelings away and bury them.

I finished all of the final arrangements, trying not to think of Benjamin and what went on between us. I ate a plate of fruit, not feeling too hungry. Decidedly, I went out to the cemetery and sat upon my favorite bench under my favorite tree. No one was visiting now, and so I was alone. I took out my handkerchief and cried until I could not cry anymore. As I finally put myself together, I realized I had to cry Benjamin out of my mind; and, hopefully, I did just that. I owed it to my sister. Astra, did I really owe her anything with all of the accusations she put upon me about our mother—probably not. The person I owed was Papa. This was his wish for her to marry Benjamin, and I had to abide by it. Faithfully, I would abide by it for Papa.

As I was looking straight ahead, I heard a noise behind me. Turning around, I saw Berenice. "Hello dear friend, have a seat," I motioned on the bench, quickly wiping my eyes hoping she would not see.

"Thank you, Asphodel. I was taking a short cut through the cemetery to go to the park. I did not think I would find you here right now. Have you been crying?" She asked concerned, realizing I must look a mess.

"Yes, I have, over something I cannot do anything about, so I will live with a secret for the rest of my life." I explained.

Berenice replied, "I am always here for you. If you want to share the secret to get it off your chest, I will listen. I do understand if it is something you may never repeat."

"Thank you, Berenice. You are such a wonderful friend. I have a little time this afternoon because I finished my work early. Could I come with you to the park?"

"Actually, what time is it? I have been out walking for a while, and I may not have time to go to the park after all."

"I have been out here for about thirty minutes, and it was about 3:30 when I came out here."

"Oh, my goodness, I have been out longer than I thought. I must get home. I do apologize Asphodel. Maybe another time soon?" Berenice added apologetically.

"Thank you, I understand. Also, thank you for being here at the right time. You did make me feel better." I said with a slight smile.

"Like I said, I am always here for you. Take care of yourself and I will visit soon." Berenice said, smiling back with amiable eyes as she moved through the tombstones and asphodels up to the entry gate, waving back to me as she disappeared from it.

I sat for a little longer, hoping my red eyes and nose would turn pink from the crying where my face did not look so pitiful. I decided I had better go inside and prepare for our outing to the Richardson's for Astra's meeting with Benjamin as destiny was already written in the stars for her future, leaving me with an unknown future and nothing promised.

Chapter 15

On the carriage ride over to the Richardson's neither I nor Astra really spoke. I knew why I was quiet, thinking of the smoldering, forbidden kiss I should *nevermore* dwell on. I figured Astra was in her own thoughts of either nervousness or flight—flight in order to escape this meeting. Papa spoke with a firm voice, "You girls are both entirely in your solemnity this evening. This should be a joyous occasion. When we arrive, please put on your best smiles and be cordial. We would not want young Mr. Richardson to think you shy, or uninterested in him Astra. Asphodel, I do not understand why you look so glum, but please snap out of it. You have been working with this young man all week. I assumed you were getting along because you never complained to me about anything."

"Papa, I will be fine and be social once we get there. I am just a little under the weather, but this too shall pass." I answered him with hopeful countenance to appease him.

"I will also perform as you wish. You know how I feel about this whole situation." Astra added almost with a snarl and one eyebrow cocked up with eyes staring right through Papa.

"We will have a most pleasant evening with the Richardsons. Are we all clear?" He asked glaring at both of us.

"Yes, Papa." I said and smiled.

"We are as crystal clear as new spectacles!" Astra demanded, adjusted her wrap, and turned to look out the window forlornly.

Shortly after having our dutiful directions from Papa, we arrived at the Richardson home. It was lovely with columns outside, creating a powerful looking home made out of brick. There were beautiful azalea bushes lining the front of the home that made my heart leap. They were not in bloom, but I am sure in the spring they were stunning.

We exited the carriage one by one to be greeted by a manservant who collected Papa's hat. As we entered inside the house, I looked up to see a grand ceiling with paintings rising up high as if the foyer were a miniature art gallery. To the left side, there was a staircase that curved up to the second floor. The steps were made out of black walnut and stood out finely in grand style—so picturesque. I was mesmerized at the beauty of this entry way that I had to be tapped on the shoulder by Papa to wake up from my daydream so we could move into the parlor.

Mrs. Richardson was sitting in a deep purple velveted highbacked armchair donned in all black, her widow's veil turned up upon her head to receive us. "Good evening Willoughbys. I am so pleased you all were able to visit for our little dinner party. Benjamin will be down shortly. I do apologize for his late coming."

Father approached her, taking her hand, to greet her. "Your home is lovely, Mrs. Richardson. Thank you for the invitation."

"Once Benjamin comes down, we will continue with introductions, and then move to the dining room for dinner," she declared as she looked at both Astra and me, trying to figure out which twin was which, "Miss Willoughby, may I call you Astra?"

We both looked at her, but Mrs. Richardson was looking at Astra when she asked the question. From interacting with Mrs. Richardson during the funeral arrangements for her husband, I knew how astute she could be. It was not surprising she could tell us apart, especially since I dressed more conservatively than Astra. "Yes, ma'am, you may call me Astra. It is a pleasure to meet you."

"Thank you, my dear. I feel I know so little about you, but I know so much more about Asphodel. Please tell me a little about yourself." Mrs. Richardson asked politely.

"There is not much to tell. One of my hobbies is making tea remedies. I take our herbs, which Asphodel cultivates and create different styles of teas. It is quite fun coming up with new flavors. I do read some as well; however, I enjoy socializing with friends the most." Astra answered.

"Oh, you will have to let me try some of your teas. That does sound interesting."

About that time, Benjamin entered the parlor, "Benjamin, thank you for not taking too long. You know Mr. Willoughby, and I do believe you know Asphodel," she said looking at me. As she said this, Benjamin moved his eyes upon me, seeming to have a longing look in them tinged with a bit of sadness. I could not bear to look at him for long in fear of crying.

"Yes, mother. I have been working with Asphodel all week to learn that part of Mr. Willoughby's business she is responsible for." Benjamin replied, still looking at me.

"Very nice, I was just learning a little about Astra when you came in. Benjamin, this is Astra, Mr. Willoughby's other daughter."

Ironic as it was, I was always Mr. Willoughby's other daughter, quiet and refined, hardly saying a word in large groups. It was quite humorous to see Astra introduced as such. When Mrs. Richardson said this, Astra gave me an icy look as she always blamed me for everything. She turned toward Benjamin curtseying, while he bowed and took her hand. "Miss Willoughby, it is so very nice to finally meet you." Benjamin stated, looking at her, and then surreptitiously cutting his eyes toward me.

Astra looked at me, and then refocusing quickly on him, "Likewise, Mr. Richardson."

At that moment, dinner was announced, and we moved into the dining room. Dinner was quite scrumptious with pork tenderloin, apple slices, potatoes, and carrots. Mrs. Richardson sat at one end of the table, while Papa was seated at the other end. Benjamin was seated next to Astra while I sat across from them. During dinner, Mrs. Richardson and Papa did most of the talking. Benjamin and Astra had no words, not even a glance, between them.

After dinner, we moved back into the parlor where Papa was offered an apéritif of a tawny port. I decided to seat myself a little away from Benjamin and Astra, so I sat in a lone chair by the door to the veranda.

Little did I know what Mrs. Richardson was going to suggest next; otherwise, I would not have taken that seat. "Benjamin, why don't you show Miss Willoughby the veranda. It is quite a lovely night."

"Yes, Mother." He replied as he stood and offered his arm to her as he escorted her out the door. Uncomfortable is how I felt as they had to pass me to exit. He left the door open so they would not technically be alone. As close to the door as I was, I could hear their conversation plainly.

"May I call you Astra?" Benjamin asked her.

"Yes, that is perfectly acceptable." Astra replied.

"Well, we know what our parents want for us. So, I felt removing the stuffy pleasantries would help us get to know each other a tad easier."

"I will be as pleasant as I know how to be, but let us be frank here. This will be a marriage of convenience. You know it as well as I do. I truly do not want to get to know you and I am sure you do not want to know me." She said this as she cut her eyes to the door.

"Astra, I beg your pardon, but I do want to know you, especially since you will be my wife in due time. We should make the best of this situation and try and make this work. Bringing misery into this before you have even given it a try brings doom to both of us. Am I so awful you cannot try to know me?" he asked in a willing tone.

"We are two different people who want different things for our futures. My father has also asked me to learn Asphodel's side of the business, which I loathe. I swore I would never take part in it, but now I feel forced and trapped in doing so. For the matter of are you so awful, I would say no; however, I know we both want to be with different people. I will play the good wife, especially in social circles, but do not count on me ever loving you."

I could see Benjamin's face—he was humiliatingly hurt by her words. I also knew his countenance, and he would try his best to win her over. Oh, Astra, how can you be so insufferable, I thought to myself. I paused thinking of her looking at the door and what she just said about wanting other people. She knows there must be something between Benjamin and me. Earlier today, she seemed to be acquiescing to this plan, but now when she saw him look at me, she has changed her mind. Papa will be devastated. There is no telling what Astra will do—especially to me. I know her better than anyone. I will never be in peace over this!

Out of nowhere, Papa appeared outside. I was so far in my own thoughts, I did not even notice him moving out to the veranda. "Astra, please go into the house and leave Benjamin with me. I want to talk with him." Papa said as Astra bowed to Benjamin and walked inside.

Mrs. Richardson invited me and Astra to sit on the sofa. "Oh girls, it pleases me so to have you here. I am especially excited for you, Astra, to be joining our family in the near future. I know you have just met Benjamin, but I know you will grow to know him and a love will form between you both no one can break. I remember my first love. He was so handsome and refined; he swept me off my feet. I truly did not know what was happening to me. He just happened to come into a place to dine and there I was so young and naïve. I fell in love with him almost instantly." Mrs. Richardson appeared to be in a daydream as she was telling us this story.

"Mrs. Richardson, do you mean your husband whom you speak?" Astra asked inquisitively.

Astra had broken a spell as Mrs. Richardson paused before answering, "Um, why yes dear. I loved Guy. The man I refer to was the love of my life. I will never forget him."

"Were you alone without a chaperone when you met him?" Astra asked, prying. Why would she ask that?

"Astra, you know she was not alone. Mrs. Richardson is a grand lady and would never break away from polite etiquette." I defended, trying to get Astra to back down. What was she trying to do?

"No, my dear, Astra, I was not alone. I always behaved and still behave properly. Do you?" Mrs. Richarson interrogated.

"Of course, I do apologize if I was getting too personal. Really, I am sorry. I think I just became carried away, thinking too much, and not focusing on the true love between you and your husband." Astra quipped, digging herself out of an insult.

"Thank you, I just want the same for you and my son. He means the world to me."

"I will act as a good wife to him. On that, you can be assured."

"Absolutely you will, or you will have to deal with me." Mrs. Richardson clearly clarified.

Chapter 16

No one spoke on the way home. We all went to our rooms and shut our doors almost simultaneously. I changed into my gown and was brushing out my hair when the door flung opened like a child opening up a box lid at Christmas. It was Astra, also in her gown and robe, with eyes glowing as arc lamps beaming down upon me. "Asphodel, what have you done?" She demanded as she shut the door almost slamming it.

"Astra, what are you talking about?"

"I saw the glance Benjamin gave you when he and I were being introduced. Why would he look at you, homely you, that way?"

"I look just like you! How could I be homely? I do not know what you mean. I barely know him. We worked together this week. You could say we are more than acquaintances, but nothing more. Do not transfer your disrespectful behavior on me. What you did to Mrs. Richardson was outright crude! How dare you act the way you did with Mrs. Richardson? You blatantly hinted she was a harlot, meeting her husband in such a way without a chaperone. What was that all about?"

"Asphodel, we may have the same features, the same eyes, the same hair, and the same figure, but you do not, and could not ever compare to me. Do not ever forget that! That woman opened her story up for questioning and alluded she was by herself. I also do not think she was talking about her husband. You saw her pause! There is more to Mrs. Richardson than she lets on."

"I'm begging you, please do not mess things up with Benjamin. This is your chance to live the life of a great lady and help Papa pass down his business. It is your duty as the eldest sister!" I pleaded earnestly.

"I can be a great lady in other ways with other men. Let's get back to you and Benjamin. I do not believe you when you say he is just a friend. If you do not tell me, I will go to Papa and make up a story that will make you look like the harlot." Astra threatened.

"Oh, please Astra, no!"

"Just watch me!" She yelled, walking towards the door.

"No Astra!" I screamed, tears beginning to flow, "Alright, Benjamin and I worked together on all aspects of the funeral Papa has coming up on Monday. Benjamin and I bickered with each other, but we had moments, such as when I showed him the cemetery, that were kind, as if creating a bond. I believe the softer side of closeness and the harder side of fighting led him to kiss me this morning as we were preparing the parlor. Are you happy now?"

"Oh really! Asphodel received her first kiss, how sweet. You had to steal my betrothed to do it, too. I am sure he felt sorry for you. I want you to know, I had succumbed to going through meeting him, getting to know him; basically, giving him a chance to become my husband. However, when I saw the glance he gave you, I was determined to make your life and his life as miserable as I could. How will I do it? I will marry him, but in name only. I will learn what you do, but never help you. You and he will have to work together for the rest of our existence fighting your so called "feelings" you have for one another. What will I be doing? Everything I do now, staying away from this miserable death house!"

"That is not fair to Benjamin! Forget me, but do not do this to him, or to Papa."

"Watch me!" Astra yelled and stormed out of my room. I crumbled onto the bed crying profusely and thinking I should never have told her about the kiss. In total devastation, I cried myself asleep.

Chapter 17

Saturday and Sunday were uneventful, except for the final touches on the Jenson funeral. While I was not working on those details, I stayed out in the garden or the cemetery working on herb harvests and weeding around tombstones. I wanted to be as far away from Astra as possible, and even Benjamin. As my luck would have it, Papa had claimed him for undertaking duties, which kept us both apart for all of Saturday. They made themselves available while the wake went on in the parlor. Papa really wanted me to assist, but I insisted I work outside. I even kept my lunch time earlier so to avoid any encounters.

On Sunday after church, I put on one of my work dresses because the front part of the cemetery was overdue for weeding. My asphodels looked shabby, and with the funeral tomorrow, I could not have people coming into the cemetery and seeing such a fright. I weeded all afternoon, leaving the front area looking pristine and like delightful death. There was nothing more exquisite than the asphodels against the tombstones. "The grass was short, springy, sweet-scented, and Asphodel-interspersed." I uttered this quote aloud from Edgar A. Poe's short story, *The Island of the Fay*. Poe's words always echoed in my mind when I thought of my asphodels.

I perused the area to ensure I did not miss any weeds. Realizing I had, I gathered my tools beginning to crawl over to the spot. A ringlet of hair fell down in my face. I tucked it back in only to find I had dirt in my hair and on my face. I reminded myself; I must wear a hat. I continued to crawl like a *gold-bug* when I came upon two feet standing before me as I was looking down at the grass beneath me. Looking up, the sun shone behind the person casting them in a stalking silhouette all in black like the moonless night. The only shape I could make out was that it was a tall man holding out a hand when he spoke jovially, "Asphodel, leave the skulking on the ground for young boys in their knickers."

At the voice, I knew exactly who it was—Benjamin.

I laughed out loud and replied, "Good afternoon, Benjamin. Someone has to weed all these flowers, and as I have told you, I enjoy it. Besides, we do not have any young boys in knickers on hand."

"In due time, you never know." At that, I took his hand, which was warm to the touch, welcoming and strong, as he pulled me up faster than I imagined where it almost put me in close contact with him. I stepped back hastily to avoid that situation and almost fell backwards. Then, he had to catch me, which put us in close proximity anyhow.

"Thank you, I just lost my footing, silly me."

"Your father gave me a break from the wake, so I decided to take a walk in the cemetery to rest my mind. I had no idea where you were today, and I did not think I would find you here. I thought you might have gone into town with Astra, truthfully." He suggested.

"Oh no, we hardly ever do that. She goes her own way as you have seen."

"Quite." Benjamin said sarcastically.

As I stood there for a moment, I realized my hair fell again, hanging on my filthy cheek. I tried to think of something to say, but I was a loss for words. I could feel him staring at me and he still looked like a shadow. I finally looked up at his face, still silently supposing. He gently moved my hair behind my ear, softly stroking my cheek as he moved, effecting tantalizing tingles on my skin that resonated through me with fervor and unintended warmness. Unknowingly, I tilted my head and closed my eyes at his touch when I heard a voice that was not his.

"Well, good afternoon dear sister and my dearly betrothed. How are we today?" Astra smugly asked.

"Hello Astra, I was just taking a walk when I ran across your sister. I was just helping her up. How might you be today?" Benjamin answered.

"I am doing well. After I went with the family to church, I left them and went to see a friend to have lunch. We had a lovely time. I spoke to Papa, and he told me you were taking a walk. I came to find you."

"Asphodel, if you do not need anything else, I'll walk your sister back up to the house."

"I will be fine. You two go and enjoy each other's company." I added. Benjamin gave his arm to Astra as she took it, and they began the walk back to the house. I was very glad I had my back to Astra when she startled me. My face would have continued to give away my feelings for Benjamin. I must do something to remove these feelings, but what?

I continued to work for another hour, knowing I would need a full bath before dinner. Still on the ground, I heard the cemetery gate. I sat up to look around to see a nice-looking older gentleman walking toward me. He was close to sixty, handsome, confident in his gait, graying temples, and a kind face. "Young lady, would you help me please?" He asked kindly.

"Yes sir, what might that be? Are you looking for a particular grave?" I answered his question with a question.

"Exactly, I heard there were some Richardson's buried here. Would you mind showing me to their family plot?" He seemed anxious as he asked his question.

"Please follow me. The most recent Richardson to be buried here was Guy de Vere Richardson. There are also some cousins of the late Mr. Richardson who are buried in the same area. Did you know them?"

"Yes, I am a distant relative."

We walked a little further and I stopped when we arrived at the Richardson graves. "Are you visiting Spencerton, or do you live here?" I quizzed.

"Oh no, I live here, closer than you realize. I just do not get out much, but I wanted to see these graves to know that these Richardson family members were at rest. It heals my soul to know. Did you know any of them?"

"I only know the Richardson's who are left, Mrs. Lenore Richardson and her son Benjamin. Benjamin is actually here as an apprentice to my father. Would you like to meet him?"

"Oh no, not right now. I have to go back to my place. How is this young man getting on?" He insisted.

"He is doing very well, and he will be such a help to my father. You could say he is a blessing."

"That warms me inside. Thank you for telling me. What is your name?"

"My name is Asphodel."

"Oh, I thought maybe you were the twin, Astra."

This made me shiver a little. How would he know her? "Have you met Astra before?"

"No, but I heard she was going to marry young Benjamin, and I heard she was a twin. I am so sorry for my mistake, and I am so sorry to keep you from your work. I must go."

"No, I am sorry. Please stay and I will leave you at peace with your family here."

"You are such a sweet, innocent child. I can tell. Please be careful with those close to you. Some do not have your best interests at heart. Be careful, sweet girl. I have to go." He said ominously and ran for the gate.

I ran after him, but as soon as I reached the gate, he was gone, vanishing into thin air. Who was he? "Sir, you didn't leave your name. Please come back!" I yelled out, but there was *only this, and nothing more*.

Chapter 18

The funeral of Mr. Jenson came and went as fast as a cougar could run. At breakfast the next day after the funeral, Papa and I were alone to our meal as Astra was still in bed. My father spoke, "Asphodel, for the rest of the week, I will be working closely with Benjamin preparing him to take a lead role when our next body comes in. I have asked Astra to be available to be at the house for dinner every night this week because I want the two of them to get better acquainted. She has agreed to do this. The only thing I ask of you is to clear yourself away from the parlor or the veranda so they may have some privacy. I will act as their chaperone.

I pondered this for a long moment, longer than I realized because Papa was snapping his fingers to bring me out of my thoughts. "Asphodel, what say you?"

"I would like to go and stay with Cousin Lucy for the week. You do not need me around with no upcoming funeral. I think it would do me good to get away and it will allow, as you said, for Benjamin and Astra to get to know each other better. May I go?" I asked nicely and logically.

"Yes, you do deserve a break. You are always so thoughtful and looking out for others. I will send a note posthaste to Cousin Lucy to inform her of your visit."

"Thank you, Papa." I said as I stood up to leave the table when my father stopped me.

"Stay until the weekend, and return after church on Sunday with us. Just a reminder, when we have our next customer, Astra will be working side by side with you."

I froze, looking at him with a feeling of dread and discomfort. "Yes, Papa." I acknowledged with hardly any energy, hoping he would not pick up on anything I was hiding. I walked speedily through the hallway to get to the stairs where I began my ascent. I was looking down when I heard her voice, "So, are you going to stay out of my way this week? Leave your precious Benjamin alone?"

"Actually yes, I am going up to pack right now to leave to stay with Cousin Lucy for the rest of the week. You will have him all to yourself."

"Well, aren't we the sacrificial lamb. When you get back, he will be all mine." She said viciously.

As she kept talking, rubbing all of this in my face, I kept walking, ascending the stairs one by one until I reached the landing and marched into my room. I packed my things quickly so I could remove myself from her, even if it was just for a week. I would always love my sister, but right now, I loathed every fiber of her being.

Chapter 19

Staying at Cousin Lucy's house this week proved to be the break I needed. I brought my books, my journal, my gardening tools, and my asphodels. Her garden always needed something fresh, so I obliged myself to add a few plants and flowers—petunias and asphodels. I dug up a few asphodel tubers to replant around her two oak trees. My second day was spent outside planting and weeding, freshening up her yard because my first day was spent resting and catching up with her. It was hot outside today, but I did remember my hat, and I stayed in the shade as much as possible. Lucy walked outside around three o'clock and brought me some lemonade as she insisted I come up on the porch for a rest.

"Cousin Asphodel, you do too much. I thought you were here to rest. That is what your father wrote me." Lucy scolded.

"Lucy, gardening brings rest to me. I love it and it reduces my stress. I just keep weeding and planting, and all my thoughts go out of my head. Now, physically, it is tiresome. Again, though, I love it."

"I just don't want you to get palpitations and faint."

"I'll be fine. I do this all the time at home. I promise tomorrow I will read and journal, and the most exercise I will get is if I walk over to the park where I will sit down at the gazebo to read and journal. How does that sound?" I asked, knowing it would make her feel better.

"Yes, dear, that would be much better," she agreed as she went to the railing of the porch to look around the yard at my handiwork, "But, oh, Asphodel, you did too much. However, it is breathtaking."

"Thank you, I knew the asphodels would be beautiful around your oaks. We have so many in the cemetery, it was good for me to thin them out."

83

"I do not understand how you can bear living with those graves right next to your house. It's too creepy for me. When I worked with your father, I was always afraid of haints. I knew one of them deceased bodies would have a haint escape out of them and mistake me for someone they needed to take revenge. You know I convinced him to paint the porch ceiling haint blue to keep them out. I always pray for you girls and your father. Creeps me out, it does." Lucy finished her tirade and drank some lemonade.

"Oh Lucy, there are no ghosts at our house. I have always felt safe, even with the visitors to the cemetery. I have met some lovely people who come in to visit their loved ones. Did you ever meet any visitors while you worked there before I started helping out?" I asked curiously.

"Let me think, maybe. Um, come to think of it, there was a young girl who would pass through on her way home every now and then. I only went out to the cemetery when I absolutely had to where I was putting flowers on a grave or removing dead flowers. Other than that, I stayed in the house. The young girl is the only one I can think of, and I do not even remember her name. I know I met others, but none stick out to me except that lovely girl."

"As much as I am out there, I meet plenty. One of them I met and became friends with comes by quite regularly. We talk and then she is usually on her way to the library, park, or home. Anyways, I was just curious who you might have met?"

"Well, just be careful you don't bring a haint in the house with you. You will never get rid of them. Are you finished out here for the day."

"I guess so. Thank you for the lemonade. Let me grab my tools and then I'll be in." I told her so she would not feel obligated to stay out here while I cleaned up.

"Alright dear, thank you again." Lucy said as she moved inside.

Just as I picked up my bag of tools and stood up, I saw a carriage driving by. I had to look twice because I thought I saw Astra in it; indeed, I did. I did not recognize the carriage, but anyone could tell, it came from a wealthy family. She was not alone; and it was no other woman in the cab with her, it was a man, and one I did not recognize. She was at it again and she would never learn. If I told Papa, would he do anything about it? Or would he still think marrying her off to Benjamin would fix her. What Papa did not understand is she was not a device that could be tinkered with to work properly. She was a grown woman who had never been told no. I want to believe if our mother were here, Astra would behave. I like to think so anyway.

After a bath and a change of dress, I felt invigorated. Lucy and I had a small dinner. We had a salad with ham, cheese, and celery on assorted greens. Lucy had a hard-boiled egg, but I did not because I do not care for eggs of any kind by themselves. We also had bread. This was a nice, light dinner for one of the hottest days of the summer. After dinner, we sat in the parlor talking. Lucy worked on her embroidery, and I brought in my journal.

"Lucy, Papa will not talk about mother that much, even though I know he idolized her. What was she like when you were young, before she married Papa?" I point-blank asked Lucy, putting her a little on the spot.

"Uh, oh. No one has really talked about Belladonna in so long." She said anxiously.

"I really want to hear stories about my mother."

"Well, Belladonna was a stunning creature. You girls favor her so. When we were young, we played with dolls together. It was so much fun. We would also play dress up and have our own little tea parties with our imaginary friends. I remember one time, when we were about seven, we rummaged through my mother's closet and found her ball gowns. We each put one on and then raided her jewelry. We had pearls hanging so long from our necks, I am surprised we didn't break the necklaces," Lucy paused to laugh as I laughed with her, "we acted like we were grand duchesses being introduced as the important guests invited from some exotic country. Oh, those were the days."

"When you were a little older and introduced into society, how was she then?"

"Well, we were not as close once we were around thirteen and fourteen. She became friends with other girls, but those girls thought I was too prudish. They were right after all; I did not fit in with them. So, I made friends of my own." Lucy explained.

"Oh, so Mother was not as conservative?" I hesitantly asked.

"Asphodel, I think your father should talk to you more about your mother." She insisted.

"I just have one more question. Was my mother more like me or more like Astra?"

"Your father may not forgive me for saying this, but Astra takes after your mother in so many ways. For anything else, you will have to discuss this with Thomas." Lucy finished and looked down at her embroidery.

I respected Cousin Lucy so much, I did not press on. I actually felt a little shameful for asking her to answer my last question against Papa's wishes. To give Lucy some peace, I decided to put all this down in my journal as we continued to sit in the parlor.

After a few hours, we both decided to retire to our rooms to get some sleep. Working in the garden wore me out. Tomorrow, I will take a walk to my favorite gazebo after breakfast. I knew that would clear my head.

The next morning, I was up at eight o'clock, breakfast was finished by nine o'clock, and then I was off for my morning constitutional. Since Lucy lived in town, I walked around Paradise Park for about thirty minutes before arriving at my gazebo. Thankfully, no one was there, so I sat down and took out my journal. Penning my thoughts always helped me work through things that lingered in my mind. How I had so many of those lingerings at once, I never dreamed I would be in a situation like this.

While my head was deep into the depths of writing, I enjoyed the sounds of the birds all around me. I could distinctly pick out the clicks and whirrs of the blue jays and the caws of crows nearby. How delightful I was hearing birds from the same family, Corvidae, at the same time. As I continued to write, I felt a shadow arrive upon me, blocking my sunlight. Raising my head, I was in the midst of Benjamin looking down on me. "Good morning, Benjamin."

"Good morning to you as well. I am not surprised to find you here as I know this is one of your favorite spots. Is it a close walk from your cousin's?" He said, sitting across from me on the open bench.

"Oh yes, it is a very short walk. In fact, I walked around the park before coming here to journal. The weather is so nice this morning, I have so enjoyed being out in nature today. What brings you through Paradise Park?"

"I had some errands to run for your father and so I decided to take a cut through on my way into town. Like you, I also felt the weather rather nice today." He answered pleasantly.

"How are you getting along with my sister?" I asked, and almost regretted bringing it up. My mouth worked faster than my brain.

"Actually, I have not seen much of her so far this week. She had plans yesterday afternoon. Your father asked me to stay for dinner this evening where Astra will be present."

"Oh, I see. She makes plans many afternoons." I said shamelessly with the thought of seeing her in that carriage yesterday, "I hope your dinner with her goes well this evening. I will be returning home on Sunday after church. Papa plans to pick me up at my cousin's house to bring me back home with all my things. I have had a lovely time visiting Cousin Lucy. I realized how much I have missed seeing her since she decided to retire from working with Papa. I have told myself I need to see her more often. You should meet her soon, I should think. I know you will like her." I added.

"Would it be an imposition to walk you back to your cousin's now? That is, if you are finished writing for the day." Benjamin suggested.

Before I answered, I considered his offer very carefully. I wanted to be near him, close to him, talking about things we both liked; however, should I just say no to discourage our closeness. I felt awkward pausing for such a time, looking into his eyes, longing to sit beside him. Again, my mouth and heart answered for me, "Oh, thank you, Benjamin, that would be quite nice of you to escort me to Lucy's."

He offered his arm as he stood up, "Miss Asphodel," he waited for me to stand up and put my arm through his, saying, "which way to Miss Lucy's?"

I pointed in the direction of the main gate of the park. We walked for a bit, just exchanging directions on how to get to my cousin's house. When finally, he broke this unnerving small talk, "Asphodel, I am still having a difficult time getting you out of my mind and my heart. Let me go to your father and suggest we marry instead of me marrying your sister."

"Benjamin, I would be afraid of the wrath Astra would bring if you did that. I also do not think my father would allow it for several reasons I cannot speak to. I am so sorry, but please do not go to my father. We just need to forget our feelings, regardless of how hard it is to let go." I turned away because tears were forming in my eyes. I had not expected this today. My feelings had not changed, but I was trying so much to think of anything else but him.

He stopped on the road, turned me towards him, and grasped my hands in his. "I will never stop feeling the way I do about you. It is emblazoned in the core of my very heart and soul," he paused and kissed my hand and romantically said, "*and the ruby-red asphodel, that its exceeding beauty spoke to our hearts in loud tones.*" I was reading the story of Eleonora by Poe last night when I came upon that line, which reminded me of you."

"Oh Benjamin, please do not make this harder than it already is. Those are the most exquisite words ever spoken to me. I must leave you before anyone sees us together; and before, our emotions take us to another place and time." Crying again, I pulled my hands away and ran towards Lucy's home. When I was out of sight of Benjamin, and anyone else, I pulled out my handkerchief to blot my eyes. I waited for a few moments and turned back towards the street where we were walking. Benjamin could not see me. He slowly walked towards my own home, hands in pocket, with a solemn face and bowed head. Before he could look my direction, I continued to move along away from him, sad and lonely.

Chapter 20

When I arrived back at Lucy's, I stayed in my room the rest of the afternoon until dinner. We ate quietly and I excused myself early, giving the reason as being rather tired from the past few days. Lucy did not question me, so I read in my room until I fell asleep with the book in my hand.

The next morning, I felt much better and so I spent the day with Lucy as we talked about family times, books, and gardening. These topics kept my mind away from Benjamin, as well as Astra. This gave me peace, showing I could refrain from dwelling on him. There was hope after all.

The rest of the week proved to be a restful, agreeable vacation from home, but I did miss Papa and my duties. I was ready to go back at this point. Saturday night after dinner, Lucy and I sat on the veranda because the night provided us a cool respite from the warm few days this week. We sat in silence for a small while, when Lucy began the conversation. "Asphodel, I have had such an enjoyable time with you staying here with me this week. Please do not hesitate to come back anytime you would like. Your visit has done me well."

"Thank you ever so much Lucy. I might just take you up on that offer sooner rather than later."

"However, I know something has been troubling you," she put up a hand as I was about to interrupt her, "Wait child, I can tell you have done some crying. It shows so fresh in your face. You did not know it, but I saw you come back from your park visit the other day. I was looking out the window from my bedroom. I saw the tears and you trying to erase the evidence with your handkerchief. Dear girl, what is wrong?" Lucy asked concernedly.

"Lucy, I just cannot talk about it. Only two other people know and I just can't!" I blurted out, beginning to cry.

"Asphodel, you may confide in me. I promise not to tell anyone, or even your father. I could tell you had no one to talk to, and you seemed so stricken with sadness. Sharing with me I believe will make you feel better."

"Alright, you promise to keep my secret?" I asked hesitatingly.

"Yes, I promise wholeheartedly."

"Well, the truth is, I am in love with a man I could never possibly be with, and I do believe he feels the same for me. He is betrothed to someone else and there is no changing that fact."

"If he was betrothed, how did the two of you fall in love?"

"We were working together and it just happened as we became more familiar with likes and dislikes. And…and, then…" I paused, not being able to form the words.

"And what?" Lucy asked sternly.

"And he kissed me. Nothing else happened, just a kiss. No one saw us. We didn't mean for any of this to happen, I promise. Now, the girl whom he will marry knows and is making my life miserable."

"Oh Asphodel, it is Astra and that Richardson boy. I see now. I am so sorry my darling. Has being here with me helped you?"

"Yes, ma'am, it has, but I'm still in love with him."

"Feelings of love do not go away like a thief in the night; they linger like an unwanted guest. Your father confided in me about this plan that Mrs. Richardson proposed to him. He is convinced this will help not only his business, but it will help Astra's place in society. Unfortunately, you are going to have to accept this. Thomas will not change his mind." Lucy said straightforwardly.

"Yes, I know, and that is the hardest part. I want Astra to change and be the lady she was brought up to be. I wish I never met him and then this would not have happened."

"Asphodel, you will begin to let go, but it will take time. What we need to do is put you more in society circles so you might meet a nice young man. I will work on that, and come spring, I will have you going to parties and balls. How does that sound?"

"I guess that sounds okay. Parties and balls do not interest me much, but if that is what I have to do, I'll do it for my sake and Papa's sake. I will not spoil what he wants."

Lucy added, "Alright then, it is settled. Tomorrow you will go back home. Your work will help you distract yourself from your feelings. Closer to spring, you will come stay with me for a bit again, attending different events where you will forget about this young man. Is that a deal?"

"Yes, ma'am. Thank you for listening. I look forward to the spring." I nicely said; however, thinking about how I would get through the fall and winter. Only time would have an answer, but what answer would I be given?

Chapter 21

After church the next day, Lucy and I came home to wait for my father to arrive in the carriage. I had all my things packed and downstairs ready to go. My father said he would be here shortly as he had an errand to run before picking me up.

Lucy and I waited in the parlor for him as we talked, avoiding the conversation we spoke of last night. I think she was fearful of having me to begin crying again. I could not blame her for that because I did not want to keep crying.

About thirty minutes later, Papa arrived and entered the parlor. "Lucy, thank you so much for allowing Asphodel to stay with you. I can tell just by looking at her, she got lots of rest. Asphodel, we have a customer coming in tomorrow, so I hope you will be ready to get back to it?"

"Yes Papa, I'm ready. Thank you again Cousin Lucy. My stay here has been more fruitful than I anticipated. I thank you from the bottom of my heart." I said as I curtseyed.

"Dear Asphodel, like I said, you may come and stay any time you like. I am truly happy I was here to converse with you on many topics. You have a bright future ahead of you and I look forward to seeing you shine like the flower you were named after." Lucy sincerely stated.

Papa interjected, "Asphodel does have a nice future to look forward to working with me. I could not do everything alone. Daughter, let's be off. Thank you again, Lucy."

"Yes, Papa."

"Goodbye you two and take care. I will see you soon."

As we were heading out the door, I looked back and saw Lucy wink at me. I ran over and gave her a hug before I ran out the door.

Upon arriving at home, I took my things upstairs and unpacked. I had a wonderful visit, but I did miss home and my room. I stayed here all afternoon putting my things back in order and then doing some reading. When it was time for dinner, I came downstairs to the dining room to find not only Papa and Astra, but Benjamin as well.

"I hope I am not late. I actually thought I was early." I said.

Papa added, "You are early, but we were just earlier than you. Have a seat."

I sat down and dinner was served with chicken, green beans, and cabbage. Dinner was tasty and satisfying; however, not much conversation took place. I felt like I was missing something. Even Astra seemed different and very quiet, which made me extremely suspicious.

We finished dinner and all moved into the parlor. My father asked Benjamin about a few things concerning our customer coming in tomorrow, and then he took the conversation in another direction. "Asphodel, are you all settled back in from your trip?"

"Yes, Papa. I had a nice time with Lucy, but I am happy I am back home. I missed all of you."

"Very nice. Well, tomorrow as I said, we have a new customer coming in, so just be ready. Astra will also be observing what you do so she can learn. Astra, are you ready for these new tasks in your life?" Papa asked.

"I am, Papa. Asphodel, please show me everything tomorrow. I know it will take me a little while to feel comfortable doing it on my own, but learning from you will give me the upper edge on doing things correctly." Astra acknowledged.

"Astra, I have always wanted you to help me, so you will learn faster than you think," Pausing to think about something she said, I asked, "Wait, Astra, you said something about doing things by yourself. I will always be here to help. So, what does that mean?"

Astra looked at Benjamin, and then at Papa. I felt like a clueless idiot, feeling left out of a joke. "Asphodel, we have some news to tell you that you will be so pleased with," Papa gleefully stated, "Astra, go ahead."

"Oh Asphodel, Benjamin and I, with Papa's approval, have decided to go ahead and be married. We have even set a date, September 1st." Astra squealed.

I sat mesmerized with devastation, what changed in just a half of a week? I fought back tears, looking at Benjamin who stared back at me until he couldn't. I hesitated to ask my voice to be present in the conversation as I gulped and quietly croaked, "Congratulations, I thought if any wedding would be happening, it would be in the spring."

"We just couldn't wait, so Papa said, why not." Astra stated with a comeback as if to spite me.

"Well, I guess that means we have lots of planning to do quickly, don't we Astra?" I responded stoically.

"Thank you Asphodel, I will need your help so much." Astra said, glaring at me with fiery eyes as if she had won a battle carrying her torch of victory.

At this I succumbed into an oblivion of disparity and sorrow as my broken heart ripped in two. I would hide my feelings for the evening and grieve in silence and solitude where no onlooker could see my emotions evolving into endless expressions of exhaustion. I, Asphodel Willoughby, will not let them see me in despair.

Conversations went on about plans for the wedding, as I decided to go outside onto the veranda. I needed fresh air. I stood by the railing looking out into the deep darkness for consolation. I knew this was coming, but not this soon. I kept to my thoughts trying to think of what I needed to prepare for tomorrow, when I heard footsteps behind me. After a moment, Benjamin stood against the railing on the right side of me. I could feel him looking at me, but I just could not turn my head. If I did, major rain would flow from my eyes, flooding my entire being.

"Asphodel, I need to talk to you. Astra has gone up to her room, and we just have a few minutes."

"Go ahead and talk. I'm listening." I muttered.

"Asphodel, after I left you on the road, I headed back here. Astra was actually waiting for me. She said she had been a fool about the betrothal and wanted to try and make things work between us. She said she would rather skip all the courting nonsense since we knew we were to be eventually married. Her suggestion was to get married right away. So, we went to your father, and he was all for it. That evening, I told my mother about this, and she could not be happier. I went along with everything, even though my feelings for you had not changed, and still haven't. If Astra had not been waiting for me, I would have gone to your father, even though you told me not to; however, she had a change of heart and I knew you were afraid of what she might do, so I agreed. It was the hardest decision I have ever made." Benjamin spoke so softly and sincerely, it warmed my heart.

"I understand. This was what you must do. In time, we all will move on. I will help her with the plans, and I will help her learn Papa's business. This is the last we speak of our feelings, understood?"

"Yes." He gave me one word because I knew he could not give anything else.

He placed his hand upon mine one last time as I turned to face him. Our eyes locked and he kissed my cheek, turning to walk away. I watched him go inside as my gut felt empty. I looked back into the blank abyss of the trees lining our property as the waxing moon provided enough light to reflect upon the asphodels in the cemetery, giving me comfort and hope for a better tomorrow.

Chapter 22

I arose from a sleepless night, crying, tossing, turning, and pondering what has changed Astra's mind about Benjamin. It seemed sudden, too sudden for Astra. She was always a planner, thinking out what she desired, and how she would obtain it, conniving all the while. I wonder if there was something in her outings on the afternoon and evening I saw her in the carriage. I saw Benjamin the next morning with no changes, but he did say when he arrived back here after seeing me, that is when Astra had a change of heart. To get to the bottom of this, I would just ask her once we were alone and I was training her.

Papa and Astra came down to breakfast seeming rather chipper. We ate and Papa laid out the plans for the day. Our new customer was Mr. Adams whose wife, Nanette "Nan" Adams, died in an unusual carriage accident. The carriage was leaving their country home just on the outskirts of town traveling to Richmond. Another carriage was heading in the opposite direction and did not see her carriage. She perished when the carriage turned over, and the spooked horses trampled her. Her driver and the driver of the other carriage survived. We were to meet with Mr. Adams right after breakfast.

Mr. Adams was prompt and arrived fifteen minutes before his appointment. I answered the door and showed him into the parlor where Papa and Astra already were sitting. "Good afternoon, Mr. Adams, I am Thomas Willoughby, and this is my daughter, Astra, and you just met my other daughter, Asphodel. We are so sorry for your loss, and we want to undertake all the arrangements to remove the burden during your grief." Papa suggested as Astra stood up and bowed as we all sat down together.

"Thank you Mr. Willoughby. My neighbor said you were the best in town, and my Nan has to have the best. What information do you need to know?" He said solemnly.

"Well, I will discuss the arrangements for her body after my daughters speak to you about invitations, cards, flowers, etc." Papa reassured him.

"Mr. Adams, approximately how many invitations would you like to send?" I asked.

"I really do not know. Everybody loved Nan. She was such a unique lady, almost otherworldly because she could sing, sew, read, you name it, she could do it. I guess around one hundred because we have a pretty good-sized congregation. I'd hate to leave anybody out."

"Thank you, if you would just fill out this card. I will go to the printer after I write everything up and we will have these out by tomorrow morning. What church did you attend? We can retrieve addresses of the parishioners from them."

"Oh, we go to St. Edwards Presbyterian."

"Now, what type of flowers would you like for your wife?" I asked.

"She loved violets. Nothing else will do, purple violets." Mr. Adams insisted.

"Fine, those are lovely flowers for what sounds like a lovely lady," I complimented, "Thank you again, and I will take that card. If you think of anything else, we are here for you. Papa, Astra and I will go and get to work now."

"Thank you girls." Papa stood up, as well as Mr. Adams, as we left for the office.

Astra pulled up a chair next to mine and watched what I was doing. I showed her different examples for the invitations, choosing the one I thought most appropriate for Mrs. Adams. "I like to choose different ones based on the person when the loved one tells us a little about the deceased. They always do because it helps in their grieving process."

"I see. Can you pick a wrong one?" Astra asked.

"Um, not really. Just some are more appropriate than others. You will know when you do a few of these. Now, I am going to write up exactly what it will say, making sure of the correct spelling of names with the proper dates. That is why I take notes the entire time I speak to a customer. If it is an uncommon name, I always have them check my spelling." I added as I wrote out the invitation and then moved on to writing out the funeral card. I explained to Astra what those were for as I finished up.

"Astra, are you ready to head to town?"

"Oh, you want me to go with you?"

"Well, yes. That is part of your training. Besides, you need to know where the printer is located, and you need to meet Mr. Meredith. We also need to go by the flower shop to order the violets."

"Asphodel, after we order the violets, may we look at wedding flowers? Do we have time?" Astra asked eagerly.

As soon as she asked this, my mind went to Benjamin. I had to think, maybe she was turning over a new leaf, but I would always be skeptical of Astra. "Sure, we have time. Mr. Meredith usually has everything printed in a few hours, so maybe we could do some other shopping and just stay in town until the printing is finished. How does that sound?"

"I think that sounds wonderful. Let me get my reticule." Astra ran past me up the stairs to her room as I already had mine in the office. I heard footsteps in the hall, so I peeked out to see Benjamin walking into the parlor. So, we would not run into each other, I went to the front door to wait for Astra who met me there right as I was opening the door.

I paused thinking of how long we would be in town. "Astra, I believe we should eat lunch in town because we won't be back until around four o'clock or even a little after. Do you mind going and telling Winnie?"

"Not at all." She agreed and headed to the kitchen. I went outside to wait for her. It was warmer today, but we had work to do. I glanced back at the house because I heard a noise, which I thought was Astra, but what I heard was a window opening. Standing there through the glass panes was Benjamin, looking as handsome as ever. He nodded his head with a beaming smile. I nodded back, slightly smiling and turning away. About that time, Astra flew out the front door also seeing Benjamin through the window where she winked at him, and he graciously nodded like a gentleman. We began our walk into town as I could feel the warm eyes of *a gallant knight, in sunshine and in shadow* watching us saunter off.

At the beginning of our walk, we did not talk too much. I was waiting for the right time to ask either what the change of heart was about Benjamin or why have the wedding so quickly. Astra seemed in great spirits, not fussing or fighting with me. She was actually pleasant for a change. I liked this version of Astra. Since she seemed to be a lamb instead of a lion, I went in for the kill. "Astra, I was happy to see you had a change of heart towards Benjamin. Did something happen to cause you to feel differently?"

"I was waiting for you to bring this up and I wondered how long it would take you. There was no big event, per se, but I just realized Papa was trying to look out for my best interests and Benjamin is nice enough and handsome enough. So, I figured I do not have too much to lose."

"Astra, Benjamin is not one of your trifles to play with and then tire of playing with him, especially when you two are married."

"Don't you think I know that. I am trying to honor Papa. He has always said I need to settle down, marry, and have a family. So, he created a situation where I could do that easily. As soon as Benjamin and I are wed, I want to start a family immediately. I think a child will be a wonderful thing to have."

"Any time we have been around children, you say you loathe them. Why not get to know your husband first before bringing an innocent child into the world?"

"We will grow to know each other as we go along. It is really none of your business when I decide to have a child of my own, so butt out. That will be between Benjamin and me." Astra spouted.

I could not fathom this change in her. It just did not add up how she was acting. I hope I was overreacting. I decided to ask her about the carriage. "Last week on Tuesday in the late afternoon, I believe, I was working in Cousin Lucy's garden when a carriage passed by her house. I noticed a man and a woman seated in the cab together without a chaperone. The young lady looked just like you."

"Oh, you did, did you? Well, I did have plans that day in the afternoon and evening."

"So, was it you?" I blatantly asked.

"Yes, I am not going to lie to you at this point. It was me and I was with Alfred. We were going for a…late lunch." She confessed.

"That was almost dinner time. Where did you go after dinner?"

"It is really none of your business, but we stayed at the restaurant until six o'clock and then we went over to the outskirts on that side of town to a place where we could just talk."

"Why not bring him to our house?" I continued.

"Because we had some things to discuss."

"So, where did you go?"

"I should not even tell you this because you will get the wrong idea, but we went to the Harkreader Hotel. We sat in the lobby and talked."

"Astra, if anyone we know saw you there, your reputation is as good as done. What was so important you had to risk that?"

"Don't talk to me about reputation. I have done this before and no one has seen me, so you can wash that out of your mind. What we talked about is my secrets to keep and that is that! The only thing I will tell you is that Alfred is no longer in the picture. We broke up for good."

"Are you okay with that?" I compassionately asked.

"Yes, I realized after this happened, Benjamin would make a fine husband, which I told him the very next day."

"I thought you had another beau. What's his name?"

Astra responded, "Christopher. I sent him away a bit ago. I thought Alfred and I wanted the same things, but come to find out, we didn't."

"I'm sorry about Alfred. Now that you have made this commitment to Benjamin, you must go through with it." I implored.

"I will, everything I have depends on it." Astra said mysteriously.

I decided not to pry any longer and let it go. It seemed to me she was hiding something, but I could not figure out what. Maybe she would confess all with a little time. I would be spending more time with her as I trained her and more time with her planning the wedding. This might throw me over the cliff.

We arrived at the printer and Mr. Meredith promised to have the invitations ready by four o'clock. So, we left for the flower shop, The Enchanted Garden, where I ordered the violets to place on Mrs. Adam's coffin. While I was ordering, Astra was looking at all the flowers they had. "Asphodel, I think I want to have lilies."

"I can't believe you don't want your namesake?" I suggested.

"I did not think of that. I could have astras and asphodels." She said excitedly.

Was she suggesting both as an insult to me or was she being nostalgic? It was hard to say with her based on her actions and words the past two days. "Why don't you have astras and lilies. Astras come in different colors like pink and then pair them up with white lilies. They would be so beautiful together."

"I like that idea. We can always add asphodels if I change my mind since we have an abundance of them at home." Astra stating, not giving up the idea of my namesake.

"Well, let's order them while we are here and then we can have lunch."

She agreed. We went to our tea shop, Anna Marie's, to have lunch. Their little sandwiches were light and delicate always paired with just the right style of tea. After we ate, we went to the dress shop where Astra spent the most time working with Madame White. They took her measurements and selected the style and then the fabrics. Astra wanted me to have a new dress as well, so we chose fabric and a similar style dress I had before because it suited me well. The fabric for her dress was a white silk with sheer lace sleeves. She would have a jacket style bodice with a high neck. The skirt would have layers of ruffles down the front with a slight train draped from a small bustle on the back. My dress would also be a high-necked jacket style with a bustled skirt with no ruffles and no train— basically more simplified and in a pale pink. The dressmaker assured us everything would be ready before the wedding date.

Once we were finished, we went back to Mr. Meredith's and picked up the invitations and headed home. "Astra, we need to go ahead and get these addressed before dinner."

"Asphodel, I am tired from all this walking and shopping, could you please do them this time? I will help on the next one."

"Sure, I will do these this time." I answered sweetly. She had been on her best behavior today where she did not go into some kind of rant, and she is just learning. I am a little tired, but she acted like she walked ten miles. I will give in this one time.

We made it back home. I went to the office to work, and she went to her room to lie down. Papa came in to see how everything was moving along with training Astra. "So, how did it go today?"

"Perfectly fine. She was pleasant and seemed eager to learn. After we went to the printer and flower shop, we had lunch and then we went to the dressmaker. She said she was tired, so she went to her room as soon as we arrived home. I'm addressing the Adams' invitations now."

"She usually has more energy than that. Well, I guess with all this excitement about the wedding, she possibly overdid it. We'll give her a pass today. Thank you, Asphodel for being patient with her. I know this is a daunting task."

"You are welcome. Actually, for the most part, she seemed like her old self, before she grew up too quickly. I enjoyed my time with her today. I hope I continue to enjoy it."

"I do as well." Papa agreed.

Dinner was a little later this evening, and Benjamin was not present. His mother wanted him home to catch up with everything coming up so soon. The house was quiet the entire evening, and for that, I was glad. I needed to be by myself in my own misery. I felt as though I was play acting being happy for Astra and Benjamin. I kept reminding myself, I had to let go.

Chapter 23

The rest of this week and the first part of the next moved quickly with the Adams' funeral and continuing to train Astra. She seemed to be taking everything seriously, but on some days, she would say she had an appointment and leave for town for a few hours and then return close to dinner time. I confronted her about seeing other men, but she imperatively denied it; however, she would not tell me where she was going.

On one occasion, she left right after breakfast and came back after lunch. I pulled her into the office to discuss this with her. "Astra, where have you been, we have a new customer coming this afternoon and I needed you to assist me in the parlor this morning."

"Asphodel, you know you did not need me. You used to do all of this by yourself. If you must know, I was at the dressmaker's getting my final fitting. I also had lunch with an old friend."

"An old friend? You mean Alfred? Christopher? Or someone new?"

"How dare you accuse me of that! I am an engaged woman. I actually had lunch with Christopher's sister."

"I would not put it past you to see one of them again. Why on earth would you need to see his sister? Are you keeping tabs on him?"

"No, I actually like her. I was thinking I should get to know her better because she and her husband would be wonderful acquaintances to know once Benjamin and I are married. It was kind of coincidental though. She is from the same town as the Richardson's. Her family knows them quite well. She was telling me all about the "entire" family. They have secrets." Astra said, acting like a child opening presents at Christmas.

103

"Astra, I hope the information you learned will be kept in that brain of yours. Mrs. Richardson and Benjamin are some of the nicest people around." I insisted.

"Oh, I am not going to tell. At least, not right now." She said with a wry smile walking away to the stairs.

I decided to let her go and not force her to stay with me and work. I went back to finishing up the list for the wedding when I heard a knock at the door. I did not hear anyone moving to the door when the knock came again, louder and quicker than before. I walked through the hallway to turn the knob, when they were in the middle of knocking a third time. "I am sorry we did not come post haste. How may I help you?" I inquired as I thought this gentleman looked familiar.

"Miss Asphodel, I'm Johnny who works for your Cousin, Lucy McClemore."

"Yes Johnny, I am so sorry I forgot your name. What may I help you with?"

"Oh Miss, Mrs. McClemore is terribly sick. I have come to get you or your father. She is asking for you both."

"Johnny, come right in and wait in the parlor. Let me get my father."

I had to find Papa, but where was he? I found Winnie and she said he was down in the basement with Mr. Benjamin. I flew down the stairs to find them doing some work to prepare for our next body.

"Papa, Johnny, the man who works for Cousin Lucy, is here. He said she is ill and has been asking for you and me. He is in the parlor now."

Papa, Benjamin, and I moved hastily back up the stairs speedily moving into the parlor. "Hello Johnny. What is happening with Lucy?"

"She took ill sir. The doctor is there with her now. He sent me to fetch you and Miss Asphodel. Please come back with me."

"Absolutely, Benjamin, I am afraid I am going to need a huge favor." Papa stated.

"Anything, sir."

"Please stay here and meet with our new customer when they arrive. I have confidence in you making all the arrangements. Have Winnie get Astra and she may assist you. I need Asphodel with me; better yet, Lucy needs Asphodel."

"Anything for Aspho...anything for the family, sir." Benjamin added courteously.

"Asphodel, meet Johnny and me out front. We will take the carriage. Thank you Benjamin." Papa said as he and Johnny flew outside to get the carriage.

I was about to walk out the front door when Benjamin stopped me. "Asphodel, I am so sorry about Lucy. I hope she will be okay." He thoughtfully said as he grabbed my hand.

"Thank you, Benjamin." I replied sincerely as I reached up to touch his cheek. With his other hand, he placed it over my other hand. He kissed the inside of it and embraced me. He was warm and I was comforted in his arms. I wish I could have stayed there forever.

"You must go. Your father will be outside before you know it. Astra and I will take care of everything here."

I looked at him as he closed the door behind me. Papa was just coming up the path. I ran out to leap into the carriage as we sped away. I could see Benjamin watching out the window after us.

Chapter 24

We arrived at Lucy's faster than I had ever traveled. Johnny helped us out of the carriage. We ran up the walkway to the porch as Johnny put the carriage away. The door was unlocked and we went straight in. Papa tried to find her maid, Mary, to see what was going on or if she had heard any news. He was calling out her name like a madman when she finally came out of the kitchen.

"Mary, how is Lucy?" Papa asked nervously.

"Sir, she is very sick. The doctor is with her now. I will let him know you made it here."

"Has the doctor said what is wrong?"

"Not yet, Mrs. Lucy came down with what seemed like a head cold a few days after Miss Asphodel left to go back home. We nurtured her, but she seemed to get worse when she told us to call for Dr. Haynes. He has been here all morning. Let me just go get him."

"Papa, I hope she will get better soon. She was feeling fine when I left."

"Some of these illnesses attack with a vengeance. Let's wait to see what the doctor says."

We waited in the parlor for what seemed hours, but it was really just thirty minutes. Mary and the doctor came down the stairs directly to see us. We stood up to greet Dr. Haynes, but he told us to sit down. "Mr. Willoughby, Mary tells me you are Mrs. Lucy's cousin, and this is your daughter, Asphodel."

"Yes, Doctor, you are correct."

"I am sorry to meet you during these circumstances. Lucy had signs of a cold, but then became sicker. That is when Mary and Johnny sent for me upon Lucy's request. I came right over. From being with her all morning, it seems she has pneumonia. We are keeping her warm and comfortable, and I have given her a small dose of morphine for the pain. Other than that, we just need to be there for her and pray she overcomes this."

"May we see her?" Papa asked.

"Yes, she is awake right now, but she moves in and out of sleep quite often. Don't excite her and only stay for a short time so she may rest."

"Yes sir. Thank you." Papa said as the doctor nodded back to him.

Papa and I walked up the stairs to her bedroom. A nurse was there to watch over her. She moved away from the bed so we could talk with Lucy.

"Lucy, it's me, Thomas, and Asphodel is here with me."

Struggling to speak, Lucy whispered, "Hello you two. Thank you."

"Cousin Lucy, we are planning to stay with you so we can be here if you need absolutely anything." I offered.

"Asphodel, we made plans. You may need to carry those out without me."

"I know you will be there with me. We needn't worry about those plans right now."

Papa looked at Lucy and me puzzled, but he just let us talk. I knew he would ask me later. "Thomas, please contact my lawyer when I'm gone. His name is Edward Stapleton, and he is here in town. He has all of my arrangements made." Lucy requested as she took several breaths and coughed harshly.

"Lucy, I will make sure all your wishes are carried out." Papa told her confidently.

She took a few more heavy breaths before responding, "Thank you, one more request."

Papa said, "Anything."

"Make sure I am good and dead before you bury me." She heaved several shorter breaths and then fell out of consciousness.

"Asphodel let's go downstairs and let her rest. Nurse, please come get us if she needs anything, or if anything changes."

"Yes, sir."

We went back downstairs, and Mary asked us and the doctor if we wanted anything to eat. We said we would wait a little longer just in case Lucy woke back up and wanted to see us. The doctor went upstairs to keep an eye on her.

We waited downstairs for another hour when the doctor came to update us. "Lucy is still resting peacefully, so I do not want to disturb her."

"Thank you, Doctor. We will plan on spending the night just in case she does take a turn for the worst. Do you have any prognosis?" Papa asked.

"I wish I knew for sure, but her breathing pattern is getting worse, and I know she is in great pain. The morphine will only last so long to help her feel comfortable. She is a tough lady, but she is struggling. We will keep doing everything we can for her."

I waited until the doctor left before speaking to Papa. "Do you think she will recover?"

"Child, I really do not know, except what the doctor is telling us. I do not have a good feeling about this. Just pray for her."

We sat on her sofa and waited. I realized I fell asleep because I woke up and it was almost nine o'clock at night. I told Papa I was going to lie down in one of the spare bedrooms, the one I always stayed in when I visited Lucy. He assured me he would wake me up if anything happened, good or bad.

The next morning arrived, and I realized Papa let me sleep through the night, so I was hopeful her condition was not worse. I walked into the parlor and Papa was sound asleep on the sofa. He probably just fell asleep, not knowing. "Papa, wake up. It's morning, we need to check with the doctor."

He gave a little snort and shook his head, "Asphodel, why are you...," he paused and looked around, remembering where he was— Lucy's sofa, "Oh dear me, I almost didn't remember we were at Lucy's. Have you seen the doctor yet?"

"No, but we need to find him and get a report on her condition."

"Yes, let me go upstairs." Papa insisted, walking up the stairs with anticipation.

As he was finding the doctor, I went into the kitchen to find some fruit, pastries, and coffee laid out on the kitchen table. I poured myself a cup of coffee, waiting to pour Papa's so it would stay warm. I sat down trying to think the best of Lucy's condition as she was not someone to succumb easily to the illness; she would fight.

After about fifteen minutes, Papa was calling out my name. I answered back, "Papa, I'm in the kitchen. Come in here so you can have coff..." I stopped talking as he entered and I saw his face. I knew immediately what he had to tell me. "She's gone?"

"I'm so sorry Asphodel." He said as he ran over to hug me, consoling me as I let my grief pour out of my eyes. As he held me, he said, "The doctor said her breathing became very shallow in the middle of the night. They made her as comfortable as they could. She never woke up after midnight, and peacefully passed on around one o'clock this morning. The doctor wanted us to get plenty of rest, knowing we would have a great deal of arrangements to do after we woke up.

I tried to console myself, but I just could not help thinking about the plans she and I had made for me to come and stay with her in the spring. I had already lost Madame Lucia, and now Lucy. The only two women I had ever considered like a mother. I guess I was on my own now with just Papa. I got hold of myself and asked Papa if we could sit down and he agreed. "Papa, we must go back home to tell Astra. I am sure she is worried."

"I agree, but I need to attend to some things with the doctor before I go home. I will have Johnny take you home by carriage. Then, send him back here for me."

"Yes, Papa."

It did not take long for Johnny to bring the carriage around to the front and to bring me home. Astra was waiting in the parlor for me. "Asphodel, what is the news on Cousin Lucy?"

"I'm afraid she breathed her last breath around one this morning. Astra, I am so sad. She still had so much life left."

"I know. I loved Lucy even though she was tough on me sometimes. She always had my best interests at heart. I so truly wanted her to be at the wedding." Astra sincerely stated.

"Oh, Astra, the wedding, it is in two weeks. We do have so much to do, now, with the funeral, and then last-minute plans for the wedding. I will work night and day to make sure everything is just perfect."

"Thank you, Asphodel. You are the best sister a girl could have." We hugged, which is not something we really did since we were children; however, I think she knew how much Lucy meant to me, and she felt sorrow for me. "I do have an appointment this afternoon, but I will not be long. I promise."

"Astra, please do not go out today, Papa and I both need you."

"It is something I must do, I'm sorry. I promise it will not take long."

At that, Astra gave me one more hug and kissed my forehead before she went up to her room. Maybe she is coming around even more than I thought. She seems to be putting family first, even though she has an appointment. I hope this was something to do with the wedding, and not an old beau.

Chapter 25

Once Papa came home, and Benjamin arrived shortly after, we discussed the funeral Benjamin had begun the arrangements for yesterday. Just on the outskirts of town, the Michaelson's had lost their great aunt and needed us to conduct the services. Benjamin said they discussed everything yesterday and Astra was a wonderful helper making notes so Papa and I would have an easier time getting started. Papa also discussed the arrangements for Cousin Lucy. She had left a letter with all the details she wanted for her funeral, and of course, she would be buried by her husband in the family plot in our own cemetery. Papa decided we would work on both funerals at once now that we had more help with Benjamin and Astra. The Michaelson funeral would be held on the upcoming Monday and Cousin Lucy's funeral would be on Wednesday the same week. After the funerals, that left a week and a half until September first—Astra and Benjamin's wedding.

"Where is Astra?" Papa blurted out, realizing she was not present.

"She is upstairs in her room; moreover, she is going into town for an appointment. She said she would only be gone for a short while." I responded. .

"Darn that girl! She has no sense of responsibility." Papa angrily yelled.

"Papa, remember, it is only two weeks until the wedding. Lucy would not want us to stop everything, especially this marital union, just for her. You know if she was here, she would be fussing at you. Let Astra do things in her good time. I can take care of lots of things today and Astra can help me tomorrow."

Benjamin looked at me softly with kind eyes as if he was thinking about my change of heart towards my sister. I could not think of these things at the moment because I had a job to do and the morning was fading like daffodils at the start of spring.

"Oh fine, that will have to do then. Benjamin, thank you from the bottom of my heart for taking care of everything yesterday. From just this one instance alone, I know I made the right decision inviting you into my family. You are a good man! Come with me and we will get to work. Asphodel, please go and get started yourself."

"Thank you, sir, I am proud to be a part." Benjamin said genuinely.

I smiled at the two of them and went straight to the office as they went downstairs. I remained in the office working all afternoon, just bringing a small plate of fruit and vegetables for lunch in there as I labored over the arrangements. Time moved so fast, I looked at the clock to see it was half past four. I knew I had just enough time to make it to Mr. Meredith's before he closed.

Walking at a greater pace than normal, I made it to Mr. Meredith's with plenty of time to talk with him about what we wanted for both services. When I left his shop, I felt a weight was off my shoulders. There was enough daylight where I could walk leisurely home to relax. I walked about a block when I noticed a carriage stopping just ahead of me on the street. I could not tell who was inside, except that there were two people. Right before my eyes, a young lady stepped out; furthermore, it was Astra. I began to fume like a boiled teapot, when I realized, it might be one of her friends and not a suitor. I called out to her, but she did not hear me right away. I had to pick up the pace before she heard me. I was hoping to get a glimpse of who was in the carriage, but by the time I caught up, they were too far away.

"Asphodel, what are you doing here?"

"I might ask the same question, and who you were with?"

"That was Christopher's sister, Ruth. You knew I had an appointment. Again, why are you in town?"

"I had to go to the printers. We do have two funerals to prepare for no thanks to you."

Astra haughtily replied, "I will help you tomorrow. In fact, you will have my help for however long you need it as long as you continue to assist me on the wedding plans."

"You know I promised I would help you have a beautiful wedding day. I am not the one to worry about not being there for someone or showing up."

"Always the dedicated, diligent little Asphodel. Well, I will make sure that this wedding will be one you will never forget as long as I have you to help me."

"I am not going anywhere. Even though we don't get along most of the time, you are my sister, and I want the best for you." I added earnestly.

Astra smiled, "I know, we will always have each other no matter what happens."

We walked home together side by side in silence. We each knew how the other one felt about the upcoming weeks in addition to the loss of Lucy and how this would affect our family. Hopefully, by the first of September, our family could go back to a little normalcy with everyone settling back into routines and a welcome addition to the family.

Chapter 26

The next few days were filled with constant work and preparations for both funerals. We all worked together in order to ensure nothing was left out. Papa even hired Johnny to come and work for us now that Lucy had passed on. The Michaelson's were pleased with their great aunt's funeral, which made Papa very happy. He felt as though he did not give this one his all due to Lucy's funeral being so soon.

The Tuesday, right after the Michaelson funeral was completed, Papa and Benjamin had the body of Cousin Lucy placed on a bier in time to begin the wake that afternoon. We expected many to attend, so we took shifts in greeting our guests. Papa insisted on greeting the first batch of mourners because he felt a duty to his cousin. I decided to go out to the cemetery and sit quietly before it was my turn at the wake. I was dressed in my finest mourning dress with lots of crepe. I wanted to wear the best for Lucy as she would expect that of me. Astra detested wearing dark, dreary colors, but she agreed to do it only for Lucy's sake. I sat outside for about thirty minutes gathering my thoughts and then went inside. I stood at the back by the door where the windows were open. The sheers were closed to keep any sunlight out, but they were blowing with the breeze like an angel's gown with gossamer wings.

I noticed Astra standing outside by the garden close to the house, looking out like she had something on her mind. Her back was turned away from me. In the next few moments, Benjamin walked up to her, but she did not turn around, even though I know she could hear his footsteps.

He called out to her, "Asphodel."

She moved on her heel to one side, but not turning around to greet him, nor correct him on who she was. I exclaimed to myself, "What?!" My

114

reaction locked my feet as if I was shackled to the floor in chains. I was frozen and could not move.

"Yes, Benjamin. Are you looking for Astra?"

"I wasn't looking for anyone, really; however, I saw you there in your mourning dress, and I could not help feeling this way."

"What way is that?" Astra said continually pretending to be me.

I should not be eavesdropping, but if my sister was going to impersonate me, I wanted to know what "I" said. What was she doing? Should I go out and let Benjamin know, I asked myself, my legs glued to the floor.

"I know how much your cousin Lucy meant to you. I want to take you in my arms and comfort you. I want to try to take the pain of your loss away."

"Oh Benjamin, you are so kind. Please, go to Astra and comfort her."

"Asphodel, I can tell she is a little hurt by the death of Lucy, but Astra is not devastated like you. I can see it in Astra's eyes." He continued.

"I want you to comfort me as well, but you cannot for Astra's sake."

"Before Lucy passed, Astra had grown so much closer to me. It made me feel so welcome to our upcoming marriage. Over the past few days, she has distanced herself from me again. I don't think I did anything to upset her. I also don't think Lucy's death has upset her enough to almost shun me."

Astra said still playing me, "Astra will come around. Just give her a few days. She is excited about the wedding."

"Asphodel, but is she excited about the marriage? If you and I were to be wed, you would be more excited about the marriage. I will marry her in a week and a half; however, my…"

"Your what?" Astra asked adamantly.

"My feelings for you have not changed. I need to say this now as it may be the last chance I ever get to tell you this. I love you, Asphodel." He tenderly said, walking over to her, turning her around by the waist, to see the extreme scowl on her face. Benjamin was in shock!

"Can you not tell us apart, Benjamin? You better get it right in a week and a half. Just so you know, I don't love you either, but I am going to do my part and fulfill what Papa wants for me. Don't count on having me be the obedient, dutiful little wife your precious Asphodel would be. Oh no, I will do what I want. I will come and go as I please. If you fight me on this, I will tell my father what you just said to me, thinking me my sister." Astra vilely spat out, taking his hands and throwing them from her waist and marching into the house.

When she slammed the door, she looked over to see me as she realized I had witnessed the whole incident. "Are you proud of your Benjamin? He loves YOU, but YOU will never have him." She cursed.

I was in shock. I should have stopped her, but I was paralyzed at what I was hearing. I saw Benjamin standing in the same spot peering out into the garden. I decided to go into the parlor to assist my father and let Benjamin have a little time to himself. I did not want to embarrass him by letting him know I heard their interaction.

The rest of the day, I avoided Astra, and she seemed to avoid me. I made sure I was not in a predicament where I was alone with Benjamin either. When the end of the evening came around, he and my father were talking before Benjamin put on his hat to leave. He nodded over to me as I was talking to one of our guests. Astra must have gone upstairs because she was nowhere in sight. I nodded back as he left the parlor to go out the front door.

Papa and I stayed with the last few guests and closed the front door about nine o'clock. We were both exhausted. I told him I was going straight to bed, and he should do the same since we had another stressful day tomorrow for the funeral. Fearful as I was, I managed to climb the stairs and go to my room without seeing Astra.

Everyone was up early the next morning eating breakfast and getting ready for the funeral. My father had Benjamin handle all the details for the day so he could grieve in his own way, but also be there for Astra and me. For both our sakes, neither Astra nor I brought up anything about the conversation from yesterday out of respect for Cousin Lucy and Papa.

We did not make a truce; we just put family first. We made it through the day and evening as we said goodbye to a wonderful lady.

Chapter 27

The next week and a half flew by like a peregrine falcon. Astra and I never stopped with details about the wedding, and never started with the acting job Astra did on Benjamin. The two of them seemed to be getting along. I am sure she was guilting him to make him feel bad.

The wedding was being held at the church, while the reception was being held at the house. Everything was ready to go for the big day to arrive.

September 1st woke up to sunshine and a clear day. Papa and I let Astra sleep in as we had an early breakfast. "Asphodel, are you sure all the flowers will be at the church on time?"

"Yes, Papa, you do not need to worry. All is well, and everything is scheduled. I'll just go and wake up Astra once we are through with breakfast. Will the carriage be ready in about two hours so we may get to the church?"

"As you said, my dear, everything is ready." Papa replied.

I smiled and walked upstairs. I stopped by my room to take out my dress and underlings before waking Astra up. I walked across the hall and noticed her door was slightly cracked, but the room was still dark. I thought to myself, she must not have shut her door properly when she went to bed. When I went into her room, I had to turn on the kerosene lamp so I could see while I called out her name to awaken her, "Astra. It is time to wake up."

I heard no answer or shrugging noises from her, but what I did find once my eyes adjusted to the lamp light was a made-up bed with no bride to be. I went to her closet where all her things were gone. I inspected her dresser, nothing there either. "I can't believe this. I don't understand." I outpoured aloud, still looking around for clues. My eyes finally stopped at her desk where there were two letters—one addressed to me, and one addressed to Benjamin. I opened the letter to me:

Dear sister,

If you are reading this note, you found me to be gone. I left during the night. I could not continue this lie I was living any longer. A little while ago, I told you Alfred and I were through, which was true. I won't go into the details of our breakup, but let's say it was over something quite overwhelming for him. So, I had no choice, but to agree to marry Benjamin.

Two days ago, when I was in town for my last fitting, Alfred saw me going into the dressmakers. He waited for me. When I came out, he took me somewhere private where we made up and he asked me to marry him. I said yes and he helped me make all these plans to leave without anyone knowing.

Since you will be reading this on the morning of September 1st, please congratulate me as I became Mrs. Alfred Griswold last night. To be proper, he insisted before we left town, we must be man and wife. Please let Papa down easily. I know he was counting on me. I do not know where we will decide to live, but Alfred has all the means to take care of me. I do not know how long it will be before I see you again, but please give my other letter to Benjamin. I hope my letter to him explains everything and may he find whatever he means to find for himself, and maybe even with you. You two deserve each other! Unfortunately, that is not a compliment.

With bitter love,

Your sister, Astra

I sat down on the bed, staring at the letter dumbfounded. I could not believe she would do this. Pausing at that thought, yes, I could believe she would pull a stunt like this. How was I going to tell Papa?

I walked downstairs to find him dressed in his finest waiting in the parlor. "Daughter, why, you are still in your dressing gown. What is this? Did you wake Astra?"

"Papa, please sit down. I am not sure how to tell you this, or just show you the letter."

"What letter, what do you mean?" He questioned me worriedly, looking at the letter in my hand.

"When I went into her bedroom, I found she was gone with all her things. She left me a letter and a separate letter for Benjamin. Papa, she left us. She deserted Benjamin for her old beau, Alfred Griswold." I explained as easily and straightforwardly as I knew how.

"Asphodel, she didn't; she couldn't!" He said angrily as he began to cry.

By Astra doing this, she had embarrassed our whole family. This is exactly the thing Papa was afraid of happening, ruining her reputation, even though Alfred was in the upper class. Leaving like a thief in the night was no way to get married secretly where the whole town did not think her a harlot. "Papa, we need to tell Benjamin. Let me go and change; we'll leave for the church to let the minister know; hopefully, Benjamin will already be there.

My father, tears still rolling down his face, agreed. I took out his handkerchief and blotted his eyes. I hurried to my room, putting on one of my frocks I wear to work in, coming right back down the stairs swiftly.

We left in the carriage and headed directly for the church. Papa had me wait in the vestibule while he told the minister the news. The minister had some of the church workers stand at the doors outside to inform the guests there would be no wedding today. Papa came back to my side and said he would go and find Benjamin to give him the letter from Astra. He thought about waiting for Mrs. Richardson to arrive, but then he decided this would be better man to man. He left me again to find Benjamin in one of the rooms behind the altar. All I could do was wait, which was the hardest thing I ever had to do.

After thirty minutes, Papa finally was walking toward me from inside the church. I had sat down on a bench in the vestibule. When I saw him, I stood up. He was crying again. "How is he, Papa?"

"He is not in a good place. He let me read Astra's letter. I do not know what she told you, but she spewed pure hated in the letter to him for no reason." He yelled with fists balled up.

"Papa, may I see the letter she wrote to Benjamin?"

"Yes, Benjamin read it after I gave him the news. He crumpled it and threw it to the ground. He was as mad as a hornet and had every right to be and more. I thought about shielding you, but you need to know the real person we are dealing with in your sister, Astra."

Papa handed me the letter. I unfolded it and smoothed it out in order to read it.

Dearest Benjamin,

I know we should be taking our vows in just a few hours, but I am here to tell you, I have already taken vows with someone else. Someone you do not know. A gentleman whom I met long before you. He courted me for two years, and we broke up around the time I was told I had to marry you. He had a change of heart and asked me to marry him and I said yes. We were married last night before we left town.

Please do not have ill will against me. We never truly loved each other, let alone liked each other really. It was always pretending to be where my feelings were concerned. Now, you can pursue whomever you want. You are not betrothed by my family anymore.

Oh, and one more thing I wanted you to know because I do think you have been kept in the dark your entire life about this secret. Go ask your mother who your real father was. It wasn't Guy de Vere Richardson. It was a man called Parker, making you a bastard. It is quite funny how things turn out. My father was worried about how the town perceived me and what it would do to our family. I think I just saved the family from YOUR family secret.

Have a wonderful life, Benjamin!

Sincerely,

Mrs. Alfred Griswold

As hateful as my sister could be at times, I had no idea she would go this low. Staring at the letter, droplets of sorrow escaped my eyes onto the paper running the ink like a woeful waterfall. Papa grabbed the letter from my hands and tossed it down on the bench next to him, placing his arms around me as I cried more than I had ever cried before.

I cried for so many things: loss for Cousin Lucy, loss for the Astra she could have been, and loss for Papa's feelings for how Astra treated him. The greatest loss I cried for was Benjamin. He did not deserve this. His family did not deserve this. How could she be so cunningly and connivingly so cruel? At this point, I could not forgive her for what she has done. Papa held me tight and repeatedly said, "Asphodel, just let it out. We still have each other; we do not need Astra. She has made her place in life without us. So be it!"

All I could think about was Benjamin. Was this news shockingly true? What was he going to do now?

Chapter 28

Over the last week, a state of somberness lorded over the house like no other time we have ever experienced before. Papa closed for the first time in his life due to Cousin Lucy's death, but I knew it was also due to all the clandestine business with Astra. Benjamin had not been back since the day before the wedding. I was not only concerned about Benjamin, but especially Papa. What was this going to do to his health?

I awoke quite early this Tuesday morning, way before the dedicated dawn. I made my way out to the cemetery to find comfort in solitude. I delightfully discovered a festive fog rolling through each headstone like vines creeping through tree limbs. As I sat on my devoted bench, I looked up at the sky, which was overcast as an umbrella would protect its holder. I pleaded with myself to think of more positive things than what Astra did, but it was quite difficult because she, in two letters, has almost destroyed everyone I care about in the world.

The dawn was delicious as tiny beams of sunlight crept through calming clouds silently awakening, glistening over the flowers—the asphodels, reminiscent of little lights along the ground. Adding the fog into my dreamlike canvas, the asphodels exuded an ominous glow as divine as anything I had ever seen. Adoring the sun's waking, I never wanted this picture to end. This soothed my senses, giving me a calm sense of moving on as Lucy would have wanted us to. She had plans for me to find someone and start life anew. My quest would be to honor her wishes.

Just as I was in my daydream, I caught movement out of the corner of my eye. It was an area I barely tread, except to weed every once in a while. When I turned to look, I thought I saw someone running away as if I had caught him in deplorable deeds. I quickly stood up and started running in that direction, yelling, "Stop, who's there? Please do not leave on my account." It was a little way off from my bench, so I had to dodge in and out of headstones carefully. I was looking ahead still calling out to this person, when I lost my footing from a tree limb. I fell flat on the ground. I was only halfway to where who I think was a man was when he started running away.

I had fallen forward; fortunately, catching myself on my hands and forearms. I stopped for a moment to catch my breath because the wind had been knocked out of me as I fell. Next to this hulking tree was a headstone I am sure I have seen one hundred times or more as I have walked in the cemetery. I thought to myself, this is the area where Guy de Vere Richardson was buried. I was sure of it. Resting for a moment longer, I decided to try and get up off the ground. As I looked up, I actually read the headstone—at first in my head—then, reading aloud because I could not believe what I saw. "Parker Richardson, Beloved Son, Died 1843." This made me stop for a moment, but then I raised my knees to my chest and pushed myself up into a sitting position where I could rest my back up against the tree.

When I felt rested, I stood up and walked around a few headstones, finding Guy de Vere Richardson's grave behind Parker Richardson's grave. Was the information Astra said in the letter true about Benjamin? Even if it was, it did not matter, at least to me. If I ever get to see Benjamin again, I must tell him this. I looked down at my dress, realizing how filthy I was from my fall. I began dusting the crumbling dirt from my dress. Thankfully, it was an old frock I could rinse out; hopefully, coming clean. If not, I could wear it when I worked in the garden.

I felt satisfied most of the dirt was gone; however, I now could feel some of my curls dangling in my face. Wow, that was a hard fall. I wished I had a mirror at this point. I did not want to tell Papa what had happened, and I knew everyone in the household would be up by now. Still turned toward the headstone, I heard a voice.

"Asphodel."

I knew that voice…well. Turning around to my great surprise, it was Benjamin. He was far enough away, I began to run toward him with glee, but my foot caught on that same branch again, causing me to fall again; fortunately, this time, Benjamin caught me before I hit the ground.

"Asphodel, are you okay?" He asked soothingly.

"I kind of am. I was afraid I would never see you again."

"I would never leave without telling you a proper goodbye. I hope you know this of me. I have a great deal to tell you, but first are you hurt?"

"Just a few moments ago, I thought I saw someone running away and so I began to run after them. I tripped and fell down because of that tree branch. I rested a bit before getting up. As you approached and said my name, I turned to see it was you, falling over that same stupid branch. I think I might have done something to my ankle or my foot. It hurts terribly now." I recapped.

"Can you walk back to the house?" He asked concerned.

"Let me try," I responded as I began to take a few light steps forward, "Oh, my! I don't think I can." I uttered fighting back tears.

Before I could say anything else, Benjamin reached his left arm around my back and his right arm underneath my trembling thighs, scooping me up so quickly I felt flushed. I grabbed his neck with both arms, feeling so close to him like we were when he kissed me before. As he began walking purposefully toward the house, I know I turned bright red because of my burning feelings for this wonderful man. Suddenly, he stopped walking.

Our faces so near each other made my head spin. He stared at me. He watched my face as I smiled, even though I was in pain. As he gazed into my eyes with his crystal blue pools of endless wonder, he uttered, "Asphodel, my darling, I should have already said this before I let anything happen between Astra and me. I love you!" As soon as the last word fell from his lips, his lips fell onto mine, more perfect passion, more fervent fire than the first kiss we shared. I pressed back with every fiber in my being. Our kiss lingered for several minutes. I did not want it to end. However, he knew a doctor needed to look at my foot and we would continue these kisses and embraces *forevermore.*

Benjamin and I entered the house through the front door so he could easily carry me into the parlor. He gently laid me down on the sofa, kissing the top of my head lightly as though I would fall apart like a porcelain doll before he went to find my father. I remained there agonizing over my foot and how stupid I was behaving out in the cemetery. I knew better than that.

Moments later, Benjamin ran into the room with Papa. "Asphodel, what happened? Benjamin said you have done something to your foot. What pray tell have you done, child?"

"Papa, there is no sense in becoming upset at me. It was an accident. I just fell in the cemetery. I am sure it will be nothing."

He returned with stern eyes as his bushy eyebrows grimaced like a fiend and a smirk telling me he could not be mad at me because it contained a tiny, smile just the other side of his mouth, creating a dimple. "Asphodel, I know it is not the right time to say this, but I have enough to worry about your sister, let alone you. You are my dependable child. I cannot lose you, too."

I paused before responding because I became so caught up in myself and my own feelings, I had not wholeheartedly thought about how devasted Papa was feeling. I knew he was hurt, but I just realized Astra leaving was almost like a death. She might never return. He must be adding guilt to his resume of fatherly emotions. "Oh Papa, I am so sorry. I am sure once the doctor looks at me, I will be just fine. I am here, and I always will be here. I am dependable, which you will never need to worry about me."

"Asphodel, I will always worry about you. It is my job as your father." He tearfully said, hugging me, "When Benjamin found me, explaining what happened to you, I told Winnie to send someone to get the doctor. You just stay right here and try not to move."

"Yes, Papa." The three of us stayed silent as we waited for the doctor. Every time I glanced at Benjamin, I caught him stealing a look at me. I could feel my cheeks burn with fire, knowing they were bright red like a Christmas ribbon. I coyly turned away when he caught me. All my feelings were so new, something I never thought I would experience, ever.

The doctor finally arrived, practicing pleasantries with myself, Papa, and Benjamin. Benjamin sat on the other side of the room as Dr. Haynes examined my foot and even my ankle. I felt like he was taking forever to do his examination. He moved it several different ways asking me what hurt and what did not. He pushed on my foot and my ankle in different areas as well. When he pushed on the outside at my ankle bone, I winced and yelled out, "Ouch!" Benjamin stood up to run over to me as my father moved closer and held my hand. "Dr. Haynes, that is the only place that seems to hurt, especially when you pushed on it." I responded, holding back a few tears.

"Well, Miss Asphodel, it looks like there is nothing broken. I think you must have twisted your ankle, so it will start bruising. You need to stay off your feet for a few days and rest. It will heel quickly enough."

"A few days, Doctor! Why I help my father…"

"Yes, dear child, you help me, but this is no time to worry about that. Benjamin can help me while you are resting up. It will be fine. I think you could use a little time away from the business, even though it is under such unfortunate circumstances. Do not argue daughter." Papa finished firmly as I was trying to interrupt him.

"Yes, Papa." I agreed, looking down at my hands and feeling ridiculous that I let this happen to me.

Papa and Dr. Haynes went into the foyer while Benjamin stayed with me. He came over to sit beside me, taking my hand. His fingers felt warm and rugged, paradoxically a man of both some status, but never afraid of working with his hands. He sweetly kissed my hand and held it in his. "Asphodel, you are going to be all right in just a little time. You need to rest and not rush your healing. I know you want to get right up and start working, but sometimes you just need to stop and smell the roses, or in your case, the asphodels."

I blushed again as he tried to remind me to have patience. Life does not need to be rushed. "I know and thank you, but I need to stay busy and working."

"When you are hurt or sick, you just need to rest and get better. I am here. I am not going anywhere. So, everything you normally do, I will do and assist your father. Do not fret, just heal." Benjamin tenderly insisted as he kissed the inside of my hand as he gazed into my eyes. With his last words, I think he meant more than just my foot and ankle healing, I believe he meant healing over the hurt my sister left me.

"Benjamin, you said you had things to tell me…" I started to say as he interrupted me.

"That will come in time. There is no rush. You need your rest now. As soon as your father comes back in here, I will ask his permission to take you upstairs to your room. The stairs are not something you need to be climbing today."

Papa entered the parlor, walking over to us. "Asphodel, I want you to mind what Dr. Haynes said. You must stay off that foot."

"I will Papa. I promise."

Benjamin interjected, "Sir, if I have your permission, I can carry Miss Asphodel up the stairs to her room accompanied by yourself or Winnie, of course."

"Scoop her up and I'll call for Winnie. If you did not offer, I was not sure how I was going to bring her to her room. Thank you." They both laughed a little.

Benjamin paused as Winnie came right in. My father instructed Winnie about my needs for the next few days. Once they were finished with all the details, Benjamin gathered me up in his arms, heading for the hall to carry me up to my room. Winnie started ahead of us.

"Benjamin, you said something in the cemetery, which I gave no response."

"I did not give you a chance to if I remember correctly." He said, blushing.

"I love you, too."

We stared at each other as he devotedly continued carrying me up the stairs. With each step, one by one, he held me tighter, longing to entwine our lips to become one. As we reached my room, Winnie had opened the door and was waiting for us. He gently laid me down on the bed and delicately kissed my cheek as he walked gingerly out of the room, never taking his eyes away from mine until he shut the door.

Chapter 30

For the next five days, Benjamin was allowed to bring me up and down the stairs from my bedroom to the parlor where I had to sit on the sofa with my foot propped up. If I stayed in bed, Papa would not allow Benjamin to visit me even with a chaperone, so I insisted I needed to come to the parlor during the day because I might get depressed staying in my bedroom for so long. I exaggerated so I would get my way in order to spend time with Benjamin.

"Benjamin, I have been avoiding bringing this up again, but the day I was hurt, you said you had much to tell me. I have been so worried about what Astra said to you in her letter."

"I have wished to catch you up on everything, but I did not want you thinking too hard on what I have to tell you. I wanted you to focus on healing, but I guess making you wait put more worry on you. I am so sorry for doing that to you; it was not my intention."

"I know, and it is understandable with everything that has transpired. There are no apologies necessary." I smiled, reassuring him I was fine.

"Well, your father gave me Astra's letter before I thought we would be wed. Reading it created a fury in me. I have never been that angry before in my life. I ran from the church to Paradise Park, contemplating the hateful things she said. I was raw—my heart a battered, embarrassed wreck. Not only had she jilted me on the day of our wedding, but she added insult to injury eloping with some other man. I had begun to care for her, even though it had not evolved into love. She hurt me dearly, but as I sat in the gazebo, actually where we met, I knew I must face something far worse— the information about my father. I knew I could get over her leaving me as the embarrassment would disappear; however, what she said about my father left me at a loss on how to handle it. I remained at our gazebo for two hours with thoughts flying through my mind like the winds of a hurricane. I made the decision to go home and discuss all this with my mother."

He paused here, and all I could do was feel sympathy for the pain he suffered that day. He continued, "I strolled slowly home, unsure of wanting to hear the truth or not. If what Astra said was true, would it really make a difference in my life or would I loathe myself for being a bastard. Um, I am so sorry, please pardon me."

"Benjamin, it is okay. You may say anything and everything to me."

"I know that my darling, but you are a refined lady who should not hear those scathing words." He kissed my hand and continued. "So, I finally reached my house, and my mother had made it back from the church. It is as if she knew what I was going to ask because as soon as I entered the house, I heard her call out my name. I went into the parlor, and she gestured me to sit down beside her on the sofa. This is what she said:

'Benjamin, Mr. Willoughby informed me of the letter Astra left you. He also said that when he gave it to you, and you read it, you threw it down and ran off before he could speak to you. First, what she did was the most despicable things a woman could do to a man. I can understand to never forgive her as I will not either. However, please do not hold what Astra did against Mr. Willoughby or his other daughter, Asphodel, because they were as shocked as we were. Astra was a selfish, conniving harlot. I am sorry from the bottom of my soul I insisted you marry her. I know Mr. Willoughby feels the same. I contend you should continue your work with him. He highly respects you and he told me he truly wants you to maintain your apprenticeship with him.

Now, for the matter of your father, what Astra wrote is true, Guy was not your biological father, but he became the only father you ever knew. He loved you as if you were his own child by blood. You must never forget that son!

Before I met Guy, I lived in Charlottesville, VA very near the campus of the University of Virginia. There was a bar there where I worked as a barmaid. I came from a poor family, not fitting in even the middle class. I was a good girl, working hard, living with my brother. One night, a handsome young student came in, so I went to serve him. We began talking and found out we had many things in common that we liked.

Over the next few years, he took me to dinners, gave me gifts, and told me he loved me. He promised to marry me. I was enamored by him. One evening, he was coming to see me, and I had news to tell him—the news about you. Then, my brother found out about Parker and me, and my expecting. He went mad. I was afraid of what he might do. He went to the pub and Parker was there. They went out back into the alley and my brother shot him dead, running away. I cried profusely. I was scared because I had no one, so I decided to go to someone Parker mentioned, a lady named Sarah. So, I had to take a train to where she lived. I had to ask around, but I finally found her address and went to her house.

When I arrived, I was escorted into a lovely parlor where she and a girl named Annabel were sitting. I explained my situation to her, and in revealing my relationship with Parker, I found out the ugliest truth of all— Parker had been engaged to Annabel. Their wedding was coming up very soon. When I broke the news about his death, they could not believe it, but Miss Sarah listened earnestly. She, and even Annabel, were so kind. They took me to Parker's parents where I revealed everything to them about his death, my brother's part in it, and my blessing that was coming several months down the road.

They took me in as a daughter, as if I had actually been Parker's widow. I was given lessons in classical studies and etiquette at their home. They had my last name legally changed to Richardson and explained Parker had eloped with me at school. They explained away all the sordid details that were not proper in polite society. Once a year and a half of mourning was over for Parker, and you were just a little tike, they introduced me to society, giving parties and attending parties. Guy de Vere Richardson was Parker's cousin and we became close. He had never been married, but he did not mind that I had you as an addition if he were to marry me. He actually quite liked the idea of having a child for whom he could adopt and call his own. We tried to have more children, but we were only fortunate to have our sweet Benjamin.

Darling, I hoped I would never have to tell you about the past because I left the past where it needed to be left long ago. No one needs to know about this. I cannot believe that hateful girl found out about this. The main thing is that she is gone and as a mother, I am so proud of you and I love you.'

"When she was finished, I was overwhelmed. I hugged her and told her I loved her, but I had to take time to think about all this. It was so much to take in at once. She understood and gave me time. I stayed in my room thinking, and trying to distract my thoughts I read, but it did not help. I took many long walks around town, always coming back to our gazebo. Every time I went there, I always thought of you. The decisions I had to make were: was there anything to forgive my mother for; could I ever show my face again at your father's business; should I find and confront Astra; and lastly, and the most important of all, could I come back to you to find out if you still felt the same about me and could we have a future."

"So, what were the answers to your questions?"

"Thinking about my mother, there was nothing to forgive because she was betrayed by a man, but his family took care of her and me. She did what any good mother would do—she put her child first. As for continuing to work for your father, my mother helped convince me I should. She said she and your father had a long talk about everything and your father was insistent I return. He knew I had nothing to do with what Astra did. On the question of whether I should find Astra, the answer is no. Your father and I discussed this matter. He said she has made her bed, and she can lie in it. He told me to forget her and move on. The last question to answer I was coming to find out when I found you in the cemetery. Before I spoke to your father about us, I needed to know if there was a chance."

"Benjamin, I never dreamed of falling in love with anyone. Once I embraced the feelings I had for you, there was no turning back, regardless of how everything began. I know that even if you and Astra had wed, my feelings for you would never have faltered. I was content living with those emotions for the rest of my life alone and helping my father with his business. I am so sorry for what Astra did to you and I wish I could take it back. I hope she never returns here because she brings nothing but callousness and despair."

"Asphodel, I do understand how you feel right now about her and what she did; however, we do need to forgive her in time. Eventually, she may come back here. Holding onto a grudge only grows hatred in your heart. We want love to continue blooming in our hearts with all the beautiful flowers as in your magnificent garden."

"Perhaps, you are right. I do need to work on my feelings toward Astra. Thank you for being so thoughtful."

"I just want the best for us."

"Benjamin, I do too. There is one thing I must tell you though. When I fell the first time in the cemetery when I began running after the person I saw, I landed near Guy de Vere's grave. I also found another grave—the grave of your real father, Parker."

"Oh, I forgot to tell you when my mother was telling me about him, she said she had Parker's grave moved here when they moved to Spencerton. Guy handled all the details with your father."

"When I am allowed to go back to the cemetery, I will take you to his grave."

"I would like that very much. Thank you."

An endearing smile was exchanged between us. I longed for him to kiss me, but I knew he would hold back all to be in proper form, grand gentleman he was.

"Now, when did Dr. Haynes say you could start walking on your foot?"

"He said if I could start trying it a little bit today, but I should not overdue it."

"It is almost time to eat lunch, how about we try to walk you into the dining room?"

"That sounds fine." I replied to him with a smile. I slowly moved my leg off of the sofa by swinging it around to wear I was in a proper sitting position facing Benjamin as he sat on a chair pulled up next to me. He stood up and moved the chair away from the sofa over to its home. He walked back over to me, raising his arm to give me his hand to put pressure on to stand up. I gladly accepted as I began to pull myself up putting the weight on my left foot to gingerly put down my right injured foot. As I started standing, he turned his body to the side to put his arm around my waist. He positioned himself on my right side just in case my ankle gave out. We slowly glided into the dining room together. Up until today, I had hardly put any pressure on that leg. Thankfully, it did not hurt too much. He placed me in my seat and let Winnie know we were in the dining room.

"Winnie will be here in just a few minutes, and your father will as well. I think we should go ahead and tell him about us." Benjamin suggested.

"I quite think you are right, but with what Astra did to you, you do not think it too soon?"

"I think your father will be pleasantly surprised and welcome this happy news. He has been putting on a strong face for both of us, but he needs   some   cheering   up."

"I concur then. Let's ease into it so he is not shocked. When should we tell your mother?"

"Darling, she already knows. I told her a few days ago. I had to tell someone how I felt about you."

I beamed as he said this. Everything seemed so surreal as if I was in a fanciful dream of a fairy tale, but what I needed to remind myself of was that this was real life and Benjamin's love for me was formed with true feelings and a warm heart.

As I was elated with my mind filled with hearts dancing on clouds, Papa walked in and seated himself at the head of the table. "Asphodel, how is that leg?"

"Oh Papa, Benjamin helped me walk into the dining room today for the first time in a week. I think I did rather well."

"Yes sir, she walked the whole way in with my assistance, but never wincing. We took our time."

"I am so proud to hear it girl. You will be back up and running by the end of next week." Papa almost giggled in delight.

"What is for lunch today? Does anyone know?" I added small talk to encourage my father to feel comfortable.

"Winnie said we are having some ham, potatoes, and sugar peas." Peas, my thoughts went straight to Astra. She hated them! Why was I suddenly concerned about her, was it guilt taking up with Benjamin so soon. Oh, it must be nothing. The peas just made me think of her, *and nothing more*.

About that time, Winnie brought in our lunch, which looked delectable. We ate and conversed about how things were going with the business, especially a new customer coming in tomorrow. "Papa, I would love to meet them with you. I will be sitting, so I should be fine."

"Well, Benjamin can handle everything for you, but I don't mind you also assisting. If you start feeling bad, it is off to your room for you to rest."

"Thank you, Papa. I promise I will let you know if my leg starts to ache."

We were almost finished with our lunch when Papa became a little quiet and cleared his throat. He only did this when he had something important to say, but for the life of me, I could not fathom what seriousness he would bring up. "Asphodel, and Benjamin," he looked at me and then to Benjamin, "I need to talk to you about something serious."

"Mr. Willoughby, I also have something on my mind." Benjamin added.

"Well, let me speak first, freely, and frankly. When were the two of you going to tell me, you were in love?"

Benjamin and I looked startled at each other and then back to Papa, speechless with a pause; then, laughing out loud. "Papa, however, did you know?"

"Asphodel, I may be old, but I still notice a whole lot of things. I could see the way you both look at each other. When love is lurking, you can see it in your eyes. You two really did not keep anything secret."

"Sir, we were going to tell you today. We felt you should know."

"Benjamin, thank you for being so honest and humble. I am quite a happy father seeing you with Asphodel. As I have seen you two interact with each other since you have been working for me, I could tell you two have a great deal in common. Ben, I made a huge mistake with my other daughter, and you and Asphodel both paid a great price. Seeing and knowing you two are in love corrects that mistake. I know now, Asphodel should have always been the woman for you. I apologize."

"Thank you, Papa."

"Thank you, sir, but you tried to do what was best for both of your daughters. In my humble opinion, there is no apology necessary."

"Young man, you are a true gentleman, and I give you both my blessing."   Benjamin and I grasped our hands together, feeling overjoyed. "Now, when is the wedding?"

We both blushed and Benjamin answered, "Uh," looking at me for guidance, "we have not talked about marriage yet, but I am sure…"

"Nonsense, you two belong together. Everyone knows this. Winnie, Johnny, and even Lenore have commented to me about how you are so smitten with each other. Why wait?"

Again, we both looked at each other jubilantly with Benjamin giving an answer, "Well, I guess we felt with what happened with Astra, a wedding now might seem too soon."

"Yes, Papa. We do not want everyone seeing us as uncouth."

"Daughter, there is no need to wait. I have already spoken to Benjamin's mother, and she is all for it."

Benjamin held my hands tighter as he uttered, "Asphodel, would you make me the happiest man in the world by becoming my wife?"

Never taking my eyes away from his, "Yes, Benjamin!" Even with my father sitting just down the table from us, Benjamin kissed me thrillingly, and then put his arms around, hugging me tightly.

"Asphodel, I will let the church know we will be needing a date for the wedding."

"Papa, uhm, hold on, Benjamin, what if we get married at our place?"

"Our gazebo? Yes!"

"What are you two talking about?"

"Papa, before Benjamin started working here, we met at the gazebo in Paradise Park. We want to get married there, but with no grand festivities. Let us be simple and just have our close family and friends. Then, we can come back here to have dinner."

"Asphodel, if that is what you want, I am all for it."

I hugged Papa with glee. As I looked over his shoulder into the hallway, I saw a man tip his hat, winking at me, and walk toward the front door. I blinked several times because I thought I was seeing things. This was the man I met in the cemetery a while back inquiring about the Richardsons. I quickly ran into the hallway, but there was no one there. If someone had left the house, we would have heard the door shut. I immediately went to the foyer, but again, there was no one. The door was shut and locked from the inside. With all the excitement, I must be hallucinating. I turned around and Papa and Benjamin stood staring at me in utter disbelief.

"Child, what on earth?! And your ankle?!"

Benjamin stepped up beside me putting his arm around my waist and grabbing my hand with his other hand. I shrugged it off, as they led me back into the parlor, making excuses for myself that I must run upstairs for something, but decided the better of it. If I told Papa and Benjamin the truth of what I saw, they might take me to an asylum. Mum's the word!

Chapter 31

For the next week, my ankle and foot began to feel better, just about feeling like my old self. I was even allowed to help with our new customer that came in earlier in the week. Papa only let me do certain things because he did not want to risk me hurting myself again, but he also wanted me to work on the wedding plans. I decided to go up to the attic where my mother's old trunks were stored. I was told after she died, Papa could not bear to discard any of her things, especially her dresses. How delightful would it be to wear her wedding dress? So, I went on a treasure hunt, looking for it.

The attic was located on the third floor of the house behind a closed, locked door. Papa had to give me the key. As I opened the door, it creaked on its hinges with the squealing of something sinister. I left it open, not really having a reason, but it just made me feel more at ease. As I climbed the steps one by one, leading to the attic, the door behind me suddenly slammed shut, startling me, causing me to jump. Luckily, I held my lamp steady, not dropping it. I grasped a hand to my chest as my heart, *It increased my fury, as the beating of a drum stimulates the soldier into courage.* I paused to settle my nerves before ascending into the dark, dusty attic abode I had not entered since childhood.

When I arrived at the top of the steps, I saw there was a desk by the front wall, so I set my lamp down there, which illuminated the trunks to the right of the table. I decided to go through the one right next to it. Going through her things felt a little intrusive, but I found so many lovely garments that could be styled for current times. My mother must have looked like the bell of the ball in her fancier gowns. Oh, to have known her would have been magical, especially now that I was getting married. A daughter without a mother at her wedding seemed so tragic. However, I knew she would be there in spirit. I kept digging, but no wedding gown in the first trunk, so I moved to the next one. This trunk seemed dustier than the first. When I started blowing the dust off, I coughed abundantly, waving back and forth to move the dust cloud away from me.

This trunk had a few dresses on top, but underneath, there were little trinkets she must have had in her room along with jewelry. I took each item out to look. Underneath another cedar layer, I found her wedding dress. I was mesmerized peering at it in the trunk as if it was laid out for a wake. I gently picked it up and held it up to me. Ivory satin shined as if calling to me to try on. The bodice was fitted with a sweetheart neckline trimmed in satin lilylike flowers that were hand embroidered. The sleeves were puffed attached to the dress with the same embroidered flowers and the skirt was dripping with fullness with a tier of the lilies trellised around the bottom about a foot above the edge of the dress. In the front, the lily trellis came up to the center at the waist. I grasped it to me, swinging around as if dancing on dreams of how I will look in it. I dug a little deeper and found a simple tulle veil to accompany the dress. I also found a set of pearls, triple tiered I would wear with it. I couldn't wait to go back downstairs to my room to try it on.

Setting these delicate items on a chair, I began placing the items from the second trunk back in. There were a few books I had taken out, but right beside me, a book must have opened. I picked it up finding that it was a journal. This must be my mother's, I thought, feeling astonished that my father had not put this somewhere safe. I sat back against the wall, not worrying if I got dirty or dusty since I had one of my garden frocks on. I looked at the page that was opened to see a poem she copied called "Bridal Ballad" by Edgar Allan Poe:

    The ring is on my hand,
And the wreath is on my brow —
Satins and jewels grand,
And many a rood of land,

Are all at my command,
And I am happy now!

He has loved me long and well,
And, when he breathed his vow,
I felt my bosom swell,
For — the words were his who fell
In the battle down the dell,
And who is happy now!

And he spoke to re-asure me,
And he kissed my pallid brow —
But a reverie came o're me,
And to the church-yard bore me,
And I sighed to him before me,
"O, I am happy now!"

And thus they said I plighted
An irrevocable vow —
And my friends are all delighted
That his love I have requited —
And my mind is much benighted
If I am not happy now!

Lo! the ring is on my hand,
And the wreath is on my brow —
Satins and jewels grand,
And many a rood of land,
Are all at my command,
And I must be happy now!

I have spoken — I have spoken —
They have registered the vow —
And though my faith be broken,

And though my heart be broken,
Behold the golden token
That proves me happy now!

> Would God I could awaken!
> For I dream — I know not how!
> And my soul is sorely shaken,
> Lest an evil step be taken,
> And the dead who is forsaken
> May not be happy now!

As I finished reading this aloud, I could not help thinking this was such an oxymoron with the bride having a well to do husband, but her true love having died in battle. This seemed so bittersweet—a beautiful disaster. As I was about to close the book, I noticed she scribbled another sentiment at the very bottom of the page. I had to hold it close to my face so I could see her writing because it was so tiny. Looking closely, I saw these words, "To my one true love, David, I will never forget you." I immediately shut the book. All of a sudden, I felt as though I was trespassing in my mother's mind. This was not my business. I placed the journal on top of the other things and closed the trunk, grabbing the dress and veil, descending the stairs with purpose.

When I came to the door, I found I could not open it, seemingly stuck. I turned the knob, and pulled, but nothing. I started yelling for someone to help me, but I remembered I had the key to the outside lock, but the key would not work on this side. I defeatedly sat down on the stairs, thinking about how to solve this conundrum when out of nowhere, the door opened. I was a little spooked, but I stood up to walk out into the hall.

I peered out making sure nothing or no one was there. I did not see anyone at first, but as I moved out slowly, I heard my name—from a female's voice calling me. "Yes, who is…there?"

"Asphodel…"

I turned toward the voice, which seemed as if it was coming from the attic. "Please show yourself. I am here."

At this moment, the door to enter the stairwell to the attic opened wider and a glowing silhouette stood before me as if it had glided down those stairs. "Asphodel…"

"Uh, yes, I am…uh…Asphodel." Stuttering and scared to my wits end, frozen in fear.

"Asphodel, heed my warning, Astra will return. *Thy love did guide to thine and thee.* When she returns, stay strong. *It is a happiness to wonder. It is a happiness to dream.* Dreams of happiness keep you alive and in a safe space; however, keep reality unlocked and dreams locked when you see her again. For, she wants what she should not have. Goodbye, my daughter…"

"Mother, please stay, I am not sure what you mean. I need you."

"You only need yourself. The man you love will bring you tremendous happiness until your last breaths on this earth. Savor your time with him through love. I will always watch over you my daughter. I have and will always love you."

As the tears streamed down my face, her spirit rose up the stairs, closing the door behind her ever so softly. Just as she appeared, she was gone in an instant, leaving me with questions, confusion, puzzles, and shock. I fell down upon my knees, lost in thought, letting the salty drops fall from my eyes like the morning dew dripping from gladiolas in a graveyard.

I found myself in my room—dry face and blotted eyes. I do not remember how I arrived here; I just had the memory of speaking to my mother. It could not have been her; it had to be a dream. Regardless, I must keep it to myself. Her wedding dress and veil lay upon the bed ready for me to try on. I was in an enigmatic daze.   A knock awoke my rattled state into realizing someone was at my bedroom door. "Come in."

The door opened with Winnie entering my room, smiling from ear to ear. "Miss Asphodel, are you ready to try on the dress?" She paused to see the dress laying on the bed. "Oh, my goodness, it is breathtaking!"

"It is Winnie, so it is. Yes, I am ready." I rose from the bed where I was sitting, taking off my dress, but leaving my undergarments on, but adding a nice full petticoat. Winnie helped me slip the dress over my head. She had me look away from the mirror until she fastened all forty buttons down the back. This took her a few moments, so I point blank asked her, "Winnie, do you think Astra will ever come back home?"

"Uhm, I'm not sure, but I do think so, in time. This is blunt for me to say this, ma'am, but Astra needs too much attention to stay away forever."

We both giggled at that, "You are quite right." I paused again thinking of what might happen if she returned, making myself anxious, "Are you almost finished?"

"Yes, that's the last one. Wait though, let me put this veil on you. Now, your hair will not look like this on your wedding day, but you will be able to see the picture in the mirror of how you will basically look."

Winnie added the veil, fluffing it out. She told me to close my eyes and turn slowly around towards the mirror. I could feel her flipping the dress' skirt so it would fall nicely down the petticoat. "Oh, ma'am, you are the picture of radiance! Look for yourself."

I almost felt dizzy as I was turning with my eyes closed, but once she said to look, I knew the mirror was before me. I opened my eyes, and I could not believe how beautiful the dress looked. I became teary-eyed again. Winnie ran over with a handkerchief to blot my eyes. I looked again, and all I could think of was how my mother must have looked and what her spirit said to me, even if it was a dream.

"Winnie, it is perfect! It fits like a glove, even to the length. I feel so proud to wear this. I wish my mother was here to see me. I cannot wait until my wedding day."

Winnie assisted me in taking off the gown and veil. She hung it up in my wardrobe and then exited the room. I was walking on clouds at the thought of marrying Benjamin. The wedding would be wonderful, but the marriage would be more marvelous than words could say. I could not stop thinking about all these things. Then, another thought came to mind—the journal. Who was David? Was he my mother's first love? Do I dare ask my father?

Chapter 32

My wedding day, October 7, 1872, arrived with a crisp chill in the air, but a sagacious sun warmed the sky. My ankle and foot felt better than ever, and I was enthralled to become Mrs. Benjamin Richardson. I ate breakfast early with Papa as Winnie made my favorite foods. "Asphodel, you have plenty of time to be ready. The carriage will take us to the park around half past eleven. I am told Benjamin will be behind the gazebo until the ceremony is ready to begin so you two will not see each other. Winnie, will everything be ready for our wedding feast at one o'clock?"

Winnie replied, "Oh, yes sir."

"Daughter, did you remember to pull out your cape to wear to the park? It is unusually chilly today."

"Yes, Papa, but I will leave it in the carriage until after the ceremony. Mother's dress must go out and be seen. It is the most beautiful gown. I know she had to be stunning."

"Asphodel, the day of our wedding, I stood at the altar of the church, feeling scared, anxious, ecstatic, and elated. I could not wait to be Belladonna's husband. When she walked down the aisle to me, she was a vision of loveliness I had never seen before. In my heart, at that moment, I questioned what she saw in me. We only had a short time together, but they were the happiest days of my life besides raising you girls. Your mother would be so proud of you today. Remember that, dear. As she carried you, she loved you more than life itself. I know it has been so hard not having her here with us, but always know you and Astra were the loves of her life."

We hugged for a few minutes. I was pretty sure Papa had tears in his eyes and did not want me to see the strong man he was in a weaker moment. However, he had nothing to worry about because crying did not make him weak, crying made him human. After he said those vulnerable words, I decided not to ask him about what I found in the journal. Truly, it was in the past and it was none of my business. My mother may have had a love before my father, but she married him; furthermore, based on how my father describes their relationship, she loved him and the children she never became acquainted.

Finishing up breakfast went quickly. I dashed up the stairs to take a bath and get ready. Winnie helped me the entire morning in between checking on the meal preparations from extras we hired to assist her. I felt like a princess. I always wore black and gray with our business, but today was not about death, it was about life—the beginning of the most exhilarating life to come with Benjamin. As I put on my pearls looking in the mirror, I thought of Astra. I hoped she was well and living the life she wanted, happily. Benjamin was right, I did need to forgive her, and I think I just did. Going into this marriage, this made me feel even more jovial because now, nothing should weigh on my heart or my mind.

"Winnie, I am ready."

"Ma'am, you are a piece of art. Benjamin is a lucky fella if I do say so myself. Are you really ready to be a wife?"

"Yes, absolutely. I never thought this could happen to me, getting married, but I love Benjamin with every fiber in my being. Thank you, Winnie for everything."

"Oh, yes ma'am. Let's go downstairs. You don't want to be late for Mr. Benjamin."

At that moment, Winnie helped me down the stairs and placed my cape around my shoulders. I walked out to the carriage just out front. Papa met me at the carriage with the door open. He kissed my gloved hand and sweetly said, "Asphodel, you are the image of your mother. I love you daughter."

"Thank you Papa, I love you too." I kissed his cheek, and he helped me in.

The ride to the park seemed like it took twice the amount of time it should have because I was so joyfully anxious to get there. Once we arrived, we walked through the gate and around to the gazebo. This fall day provided colorful leaves of gold, amber, scarlet, and aubergine with just a few touches of the green hanging on, but leaving the landscape of summer behind. I could not have asked for better organic décor for this day. Our few family members and friends were there waiting for our moment in time. I had forgotten to leave my cape in the carriage, but Papa called Johnny over to take it from me and back to the carriage.

Benjamin's mother came up to me, giving me a warm hug. "Asphodel, you are radiant and one of the most beautiful brides I have ever seen. I am thrilled for you to be a part of my family. I wanted to give you something to wear on this day." She pulled out a little box for me to open. "This pearl bracelet was Benjamin's grandmothers. She and her husband were the ones who took me in after Parker died. I want this to stay in the family."

"Mrs. Richardson, I cannot thank you enough. This is such a special gift. I will treasure it always."

She helped me put it on as the clasp was a little tricky. The florist from town came over to me and handed me an absolutely spectacular bouquet, containing white calla lilies, baby's breath, fern leaves, and, of course, asphodels. "I am speechless. These are gorgeous!"

"I hope you do not mind, but I picked the asphodels from the cemetery. There were a few left still blooming out. I just had to add your namesake in your bridal bouquet."

"Thank you, I am so pleased and humbled by these beauties."

"Daughter, it is time." Papa called out.

I walked over to where he stood as he offered his arm for me to put my arm through. A violinist came out on the left side of the gazebo and began to play "Bridal Chorus" from the opera *Lohengrin* by Richard Wagner composed in 1848. Breathtaking could not describe it. The next thing I knew, Benjamin and the minister walked into the middle of the gazebo. Benjamin looked superb in his dark grey cutaway coat with tales, his gray jacquard vest, his white starched shirt and cravat, down to his dark gray pants with thin white pinstripes. The florist had placed an asphodel in his buttonhole. He stood gazing upon me, meeting my eyes with more love and tenderness than I could imagine. I smiled adoringly, returning his gaze with the same fervor he sent me. When I smiled, he smiled back, winking at me, almost causing me to giggle.

Walking to this man was the easiest thing I had ever done in my life. My father stood with me outside the gazebo as the minister asked who gives my hand. Once answered, Papa raised my veil, kissed me on the cheek and placed my hand into Benjamin's as he pulled me up into the gazebo to take our vows. I handed my bouquet to the florist. Benjamin took both my hands, each one into his hands as the minster began the ceremony. We exchanged rings and we exchanged vows, giving to each other until death do us part. The minister announced us, "I give you Mr. and Mrs. Benjamin Richardson. What therefore God has joined together, let not man put asunder. You may kiss the bride."

At that instant, it was as if sparks were tingling in our fingertips with excitement. Benjamin put his arms around my waist, squeezing me into him as I wrapped my arms around his neck. I could not take my eyes away from the sparkling blue eyes staring into mine. He leaned into me as we closed our eyes together. His lips met mine with electric embers. We both wanted to remain this way forever, but we knew we had an audience who was ready to celebrate with us. As we separated our lips, Benjamin nuzzled my ear and whispered, "Asphodel, I will love you more each day, forevermore."

"Benjamin, I am yours, forevermore." I whispered back.

We turned to the front of the gazebo, the florist giving me my bouquet, our hands intertwined as one. We stepped off the gazebo platform and walked to the carriage. I heard my father remind our guests to come over to the house for the wedding dinner. As we moved closer to the carriage, Benjamin said, "Darling, the moment I saw you I was mesmerized by your beauty. Your mother's dress was truly made for you. It fits you so divinely, adding to every feature you possess. I am so used to seeing you in darkness, but today, your glow and vivacity outshine anyone. Your hair is like I have never seen you wear before. Having it pinned up so snuggly in the back shows off the refined porcelain neck you have complemented by your mother's pearls. The autumn leaves created a brilliance around the auburn sheen of your hair. You were meant to be an autumn bride. You are impeccably an angel—my angel. I will never forget the way you looked today. The picture of you will always remain stored in my mind."

I was speechless, so I smiled, blushing thoroughly for him to see my reaction. By his look, I did not have to breath a word. He knew the love we shared would last forever.

Benjamin helped me into the carriage, asking Johnny to go ahead and take us to the house. As soon as he was sitting beside me, he kissed me again, but this time he was not holding back, and not stopping. I fell into his arms with comfort and feeling where I was lost to my own thoughts because I was now his wife. I gave him back as much passion as he gave me. We would share everything with each other. We were one.

Chapter 33

We had a lovely dinner after the ceremony, where just hours later, everyone wished us well as Johnny drove us in the carriage into town to spend our first night together as husband and wife. Benjamin was a gentle man showing me his love and passion. I had no question we were meant to be together when I awoke the next morning.

We had not unpacked all of our things because my father and Benjamin's mother were sending us on a little trip to Ocean View, VA. So, we quickly put the few things in our trunk we had taken out, had breakfast in the hotel, and Johnny met us to take us to the train depot.

The train ride was pleasant—a very short jaunt. When we arrived, Benjamin hired a carriage to take us to the hotel, where we checked in for the next three days. In this quaint little town, we were able to get to know each other as man and wife. Filling our hours with walking in town and the park, seeking out secret nooks to read to each other and just hold each other close, finding cozy restaurants to dine in, and setting aside time to give ourselves to each other completely. This trip was pure heaven, but I knew once we went home, we would carve out these moments when we could because of the promises we made to each other on our wedding day. Benjamin was the most honorable man, and I knew he would never let me down.

We returned home on October 11th. Everyone was waiting for us outside the house, even Mrs. Richardson was there. They could not wait to hear about our trip, plus we had wedding gifts to open.

"Thank you all for such a welcome home. We are so happy to see you." I exclaimed as Benjamin and I glanced at each other.

"Oh, Asphodel, marriage looks brilliant on you." Papa stated with glee as he hugged me and then Benjamin.

"Sir and mother, thank you so much for our honeymoon." Benjamin took me in his arms, looking down at me and continued, "These last few days were so joy filled. Again, we cannot thank you enough."

"Benjamin and Asphodel, you are so welcome. We wanted you to have everything be perfect." Mrs. Richardson added.

We all went into the house and sat down in the parlor telling them about our stay in Ocean View, and answering their questions.

"Well, Benjamin, your mother and I had a long talk about where you two might live. While each of our houses has enough room, we decided for you two to live with me. Is that to your liking?" Papa quizzed.

"Mr. Willoughby, that sounds wonderful," as he answered he looked at me to ensure I was okay with this decision, "Asphodel and I discussed this on our trip, but we really did not know what to do, so this answered our questions we were going to ask you."

"I'm so glad! We had a feeling you would be up for that, so, I gave free reign to Lenore to redecorate the extra bedroom for you. Asphodel, you know it is bigger, which will be better for the two of you."

"Papa, I am beyond excited. When may we see it?"

"How about now?"

The four of us went up the stairs, turned right, and went to the farthest bedroom on this side of the house. My father opened the door and motioned for me and Benjamin to enter first. Papa seemed as giddy as a child, snickering with Mrs. Richardson and her handy work. My eyes danced as we walked in to see lush hues of burgundy and dark green on the bedspread for the canopy bed and curtains. The furniture was all mahogany, which all blended together nicely. I looked at Benjamin to see if he agreed; moreover, he was just as in awe as I was.

"Mrs. Richardson, this is a dream. I love it!"

"You are welcome darlings. I had the most fun picking out things I knew you would like. Your father let me see the décor in your own room so I could see what styles you favored."

As we continued talking, Johnny brought up our trunk and placed it over by the window out of the way. We thanked him and he went back downstairs. I could tell Papa wanted to stay longer and talk, but I could spy Mrs. Richardson knew Benjamin and I wanted to be alone for a little while, so she suggested, "Thomas, let's leave these lovebirds alone so they may get settled in. They have traveled today and probably need their rest."

Thomas and Lenore left, closing the door behind them. Benjamin swung me around and into his arms as if we had just danced together. He bent me back and kissed me, swinging me back up. He gazed into my eyes, scooping me up and laying me on the bed. "Asphodel, you have made me the happiest man alive. My mother mentioned rest, but that is the last thing on my mind right now." At that comment, our lips were one with a fiery desire for each other, leaving no words between us for some time.

Chapter 34

The next six months were filled with the same igniting passion we had on our honeymoon. We were the happiest any couple could be working together by day and loving by night. The in-between was spent connecting with each other mentally over books, nature, hobbies, and walks. I hoped all of our days would be spent in this fashion. Now, we did have a spat every so often, especially in our work, but that was who we were and always would be.

On the morning of April fifteenth, I rose early because I wanted to see the sun rise because the asphodels in the cemetery had started seeing the light of day and some were just beginning to bloom. Around this time was one of my favorite times of the year. Seeing my namesake come alive, pushing through winter's hard dirt as warmth would stir them into seeking life anew for another year. I walked out to my bench, not before putting a shawl around my shoulders because there was still a cold chill in the air that early in the morning. I could just see a peek of light starting its daily crawl up the sky. Colors commenced as the symphony of oranges and corals caressed the clouds; the purple section were the accompanying pieces making their parts harmonize with the lighter yellows as the sun being the maestro mastering them all together as a brilliant piece I could listen to my entire life. The light of the sun poured down on the asphodels like honey in tea, creating the wonder of Persephone's torches for those needing a lit path. Witnessing this glory, I knew today would be filled with goodness.

I continued to sit because everyone was still asleep and there was no reason for me to go back in and wake everyone up. After another twenty minutes, the sun was fully shining in the sky, so it was time for me to go back up to the house, but something kept me from moving. Nothing bad, just a feeling to wait a little longer. I looked around at the beauty before me and just sighed. I turned my head, but something caught me out of my left eye. I saw movement from the front gate. Who would be coming into the cemetery this early? I felt a little spooked by this, so I waited quietly to see who it was.

The closer they moved to me, I could see it was a woman. My thoughts went to Berenice. Maybe she saw me and thought I will stop and visit. She, unfortunately, was not able to come to the wedding, and I had not seen her for months. That must be who it is, but then a voice called out to me. "Asphodel, is that you?"

At the tone of her voice, I immediately knew this was not Berenice—it was Astra. "Yes, Astra, it's me." I stood up and moved to her. As I was almost standing in front of her, I thought I heard another odd noise. "Is there someone behind you?"

"No, sister, come closer to me."

I walked up to her and could see she was holding something. I looked down in her arms and saw a little round face staring back at me. Astra smiled at me as the baby made a few cooing sounds. "Astra, what in Heaven's name? Your baby?"

"Yes, I decided the prodigal daughter should return home. I wanted you and Papa to meet my child."

"Where is Alfred?"

"He did not come with me on this trip. I decided to come by myself. We live in Richmond, and so I took the train, and I am staying at the Inn in town."

"Astra, you must stay with us."

"After everything I put you through. I would think you would spit at me now."

"People do all kinds of things in life that are frowned upon, but everyone deserves a second chance." I said as I hugged her.

"Asphodel, you are too good for me to be your sister. I almost can't bear the thought of what I did to you, Benjamin, and Papa. I am so very sorry." Astra whimpered as the flood gates opened.

I guided her back to the house with my arm around her shoulder to comfort her. This was going to be a day of reckoning.

Entering the back door, we saw Winnie making breakfast. She turned, a little startled, because she thought no one else was up yet. "Oh, Missus, I almost jumped out of my skin."

"I am so sorry Winnie. We have two guests."

"Why didn't anyone tell me? I would have pulled more sausage out."

I replied, "Winnie, one guest won't be needing food. See."

"Miss Astra," Winnie said as she looked down to see the baby, "Oh my goodness!"

"Astra, please sit down, may I hold the baby?"

"Oh yes, here she is." Astra said as she handed her over to me.

"She? Oh, Astra, whatever is her name? She is beautiful."

"I named her Dahlia, Dahlia Belladonna Griswold. I had to add Mother's name to hers."

"I love it," I elated as the little bundle looked up at me, "Astra, her eyes are gorgeous, almost like they are not really blue, more like a hint of purple or violet."

About that time, Papa came into the kitchen and asked, "Asphodel, is someone here with a baby?"

Astra was facing Papa while my back was turned to him. He had no realization who he was talking to until I turned around with the baby. "Papa, yes, someone is here with this baby. Astra has come home to visit, bringing an extra little guest, Dahlia."

I slowly stated my words because I did not know what type of reaction Papa would have seeing Astra again. I watched his eyes. He stared at Astra and then stared at the baby. Once he looked at this sweet little face, his heart melted. He ran to Astra and hugged her, crying. "Papa, I hoped you would take me in for my visit." She stuttered as she began to cry apologizing for all her terrible behaviors from before.

I sat rocking Dahlia with teary eyes, but a filled heart of joy. As soon as Papa and Astra put themselves together, I gave the baby to Papa. He was one proud grandfather. He beamed as he looked at the little one. I went upstairs to break the news to Benjamin Astra had returned. When I entered our bedroom, he was already awake and dressing. He was sitting on a chair, so I went behind him and wrapped my arms around his chest placing my head against him, nuzzling his neck, kissing him softly. "What a way to be greeted my dear. I was surprised I did not find you asleep when I woke up. Where were you?"

"I woke early so I could look upon the asphodels as the sun rose. Oh, Benjamin, they were so beautiful in the waking dawn. You must wake early with me one day soon so we can experience it together."

He pulled me around where I was sitting in his lap, kissing me softly. "Darling, I would like nothing more. Just name the day. Are you ready to go down to breakfast?"

"Yes, but, there is something I have to tell you before we do. We had an early morning visitor, or should I say two."

"Two, who is here?"

"Astra has returned for a visit."

"Oh, so she must have brought her husband?"

"Well, no. She brought her baby, Dahlia."

"What, a baby? How old is the child? Where is her husband?"

"She just said she came by herself. It's not very old—a tiny little thing. I have not been around too many babies to actually tell."

"Hmm, well, let's go down then. How is she acting?"

"She has apologized and is very different. So far, she is a new Astra we have never seen. Maybe the baby has changed her."

"Okay, darling, after you." He said as he opened their door.

"Uh, one last thing…she does not know about our marriage."

Benjamin looked at me, knowing this would be the true test if Astra was playing a part or if she had genuinely changed. We glided down the stairs and into the kitchen. Papa was still holding Dahlia.

"Astra, there is something I have not told you yet." I said easily as Benjamin came in behind me. "Benjamin and I were married last October."

I waited for her to begin screaming at the top of her lungs, but she paused, eyeing both of us and spoke, "Congratulations, I am very happy for the both of you. Asphodel, I actually had heard of your nuptials; it was in the newspaper, so news travels fast as they say. Benjamin, I am excruciatingly sorry for my actions last September. I hope you can forgive me."

"Astra, I do forgive you. I put that in the past as soon as I could and moved on as you can see. I hold no grudges."

They all sat down to breakfast talking and catching up. The subject of Astra's luggage came up, and so Papa sent Johnny to retrieve it from town. The rest of the afternoon and evening, I helped her get settled into her old room. Papa had brought down our old crib from the attic, cleaning it up, so Dahlia could use it.

After dinner, I accompanied Astra and Dahlia into her room as she put the baby down to sleep. "Astra, how long are you planning to stay?"

"I don't know." She said hesitatingly.

"You know you are welcome to stay as long as you like, but I figured you would want to get home to your husband, and he would want to be around his child."

"Alfred is tied up in some business dealings right now, so he told me to go see my family for however long. So, again, I don't know."

"All right, no worries. If you need anything, please let me know."

"I will, and thank you." Astra said as she followed me to the door.

Benjamin had just come up the stairs. He grabbed my hand, walking me toward our bedroom. I could feel Astra staring after us. It made me a little uncomfortable for two reasons, which I could not decide on the one I wanted to believe: was she jealous of what Benjamin and I had and she wanted him back; or was she having problems with Alfred? As we reached our bedroom, I turned to look back at her door. She was just closing it. Only time would tell her true motivations for coming back.

Chapter 35

Five days had passed since Astra came home with baby Dahlia. We weren't busy at work because no one had died recently, so I was able to spend a great deal of time with my sister. She said she did not know how long she would stay, but she also had no letters arriving for her from Alfred, which alarmed me. I finally decided to ask her point blank about what was going on. I waited until after lunch because Papa and Benjamin were going out to purchase some wood for some new coffins they were making. This would give us time to speak in the parlor openly.

The baby was down for a nap, and Astra was sitting on the sofa reading a magazine. "Afternoon sister, anything interesting in that magazine?"

"Oh, you know, the usual, the latest fashions and such. What, you are not working today?"

"No, we do not have any customers right now, so I have a leisurely afternoon to myself."

"That is nice. You and Benjamin seem to be getting along swimmingly."

"Yes, we are. He is a very good man, but I know you know that. Have you heard from Alfred? I know Papa would really like to meet him." I said this in a way hoping to get a reaction out of her.

"Uh, no, but as I told you he is quite busy with work right at the moment."

"Why don't you send a letter for him to come here so we may meet him?"

Astra was looking down as I asked this question, but as soon as I was finished, she looked up, unsure of what to say. "Well, what do you think?"

Her face said it all, "Asphodel, right now is not the time to bring Alfred here to meet the family."

"Why not?"

Astra's eyes lit up like two sticks of dynamite ready to blow. "Please let this go."

"Have you left Alfred?" I figured asking her point blank would nudge her to tell me.

"I asked you politely to let this adamant questioning stop. No, I did not leave Alfred."

"Then asking your husband to come and meet your family is not unheard of. It makes no sense why you are acting so mysteriously about him. What has happened between you two?"

"All right! If you must know, Alfred left me!" Astra cried out and began sobbing.

"Astra, I am sorry." I said as I comforted her, knowing there was something else she had not told me. Anytime she was guilty of something as a child, I always knew she would either blame it on me, or it would take an act of God to coax it out of her.

Still crying, "When we first married, eloped that is, we were constantly on the go, travelling, and doing all the sorts of things I imagined Alfred and I would do as man and wife. However, everything changed when Dahlia was born. Well, he changed, he told me once he never thought of having children. He loved life too much and he was too selfish to share himself with one person, let alone a child. He tried to be a father for a short while, and then I found a note he left me saying he wanted me and the child out of his house. He could not put on this façade any longer. He regretted marrying me so hastily in my condition. He added he would provide for me and the child, but we must leave and never come back."

I paused before I said anything else. She said marry her in her condition…she was with child when they eloped. My mind went in so many directions, I almost felt as though I could not breathe. I had so many questions. "Astra, I know you are very upset sharing these details with me, but I need to ask you a few questions. First, were you already going to have the baby when you and Alfred skirted away to elope?"

She stared at me for a long time before answering, "Aren't you quite the little detective. Yes, I was."

"This next question is going to be difficult, but I must know. Was Alfred the father?"

With the tears still streaming, her eyes were a storm raging as thunder seemed to come forth, "How dare you ask me such a thing?"

"But…"

"No buts, Asphodel. You want to know if Dahlia is Benjamin's, where I have come home to win him back, so I am not alone. If you must know, I found out I was with child at the beginning of July. I did not know what to do. I went to Alfred to break the news and he shunned me. I was devasted. I would be ruined where no man would ever want me. Then, Papa insisted I marry Benjamin, so I had my answer. I would marry him and no one would be the wiser, this would be his child, born after we were wed, only a little early. So, you can stop worrying that your precious Benjamin was not a chaste gentleman before marrying you. I played along and pretended to like him, which I despised, but I had to protect my reputation. Right before the wedding, Alfred realized he still wanted me, child and all, but unfortunately, it was too much once Dahlia was born. So, there you have it, all the sordid details in all."

"If Papa finds out about this, he will be furious at Alfred. However, I do not know if I can stomach being around you with what you did to Benjamin. You were going to pretend that baby girl was actually his. How despicable of you! And don't get any ideas about Benjamin for yourself! From now on, I will be cordial when we are all together, and I will love Dahlia with all my heart, but as of this moment, you are not my sister. I will keep your secrets, but do not expect me to be your friend." I commanded, walking out of the room, leaving her staring at me with a guilty look on her face.

Chapter 36

During the next week, I stayed away from Astra as much as I could get away with where no one would expect something was amiss between us. Fortunately, and unfortunately, we had a new customer coming in to discuss funeral arrangements for their aunt. This gave me a legitimate excuse to keep my distance from my sister.

We had our initial meeting in the parlor with the family, leaving myself, Benjamin, and Papa to discuss some of the details. Papa and Benjamin were talking about the casket, when I suggested going to get us some coffee and tea cakes. I stood up, feeling woozy all of a sudden. "Asphodel, are you all right?" Benjamin asked with concern as he moved out of his chair as fast as a lion swooping in on his prey to catch me before I passed out.

I awoke to Benjamin, Papa, and the doctor staring at me as I lay on my own bed. "Why am I lying down? How did I get up here?"

"Darling, you fainted when you stood up to go to the kitchen. I caught you and carried you up here so the doctor could examine you. We had to wait until you woke up."

"Oh, I never faint. I am sure I have just overworked myself."

Dr. Haynes interrupted, "Let me be the judge of that young lady. Gentlemen, would you excuse me for a short while so I may examine Mrs. Richardson."

It was like a dream when anyone called me Mrs. Richardson. I hoped I would always feel this way. As I was daydreaming, Benjamin and Papa went out into the hall. Before they shut the door, I heard Astra walk up asking if I was okay. I wish she had not found out I had fainted.

Dr. Haynes did a thorough examination both physically and mentally, quizzing me about all kinds of things to determine what was going on. "Dr. Haynes, I feel fine now. I am sure it was nothing."

"Asphodel, I have known you since you were knee-high to a grasshopper. I have treated you for every cold and ailment you have ever had. You do have a condition."

I paused—condition. Was I really sick? I felt nothing. I looked at him as all these thoughts swam through my head. He watched me all this time, giving a wry smile as he could assess I was beginning to worry. "Child, yes, you do have a condition, but it is the best kind."

"Dr. Haynes, no condition is the best kind. What do you mean?"

"You are going to have a baby!"

It took me a moment to process this. I smiled back at him with such pride. I know my cheeks must have flushed every color of pink and red that were imaginable. "Oh, my goodness! I am elated…a baby."

"If my calculations are right, you can expect the little bundle sometime in October."

"Doctor, please let me tell Benjamin in my own way."

"Yes, ma'am. I will go get him first."

As he went into the hall and closed the door, I had a moment to myself. I could not stop smiling. At that moment, Benjamin entered by himself, sitting next to me as he faced me on the bed. "Asphodel dear, the doctor said you had some type of condition. Do I need to bring him back in to explain this to both of us?"

"No Benjamin, this is a very special condition. He explained everything to me, so I understand. This will come to pass sometime in October."

"What do you mean? What is wrong?" Benjamin cried out as if I were going to die.

"Sweetheart, my condition will be over in October because we will have a beautiful baby."

His eyes told me how he felt—they were like the waters dancing to and fro with excitement beyond compare. He bent down towards me and planted the sweetest kiss on my lips. His lips were soft, but firm, tenderly kissing me as if I were a fragile doll. I acquiesced, giving my full lips back to him as ecstatically as I could. He was my life, my love, and my all. Now, he was the father of my child, whom we would meet in a short while. The embodiment of ourselves.

"Benjamin, we should probably not keep Papa waiting. We do not want him worrying."

"Uh, yes, we can celebrate this later tonight." As he said this, he blew me a kiss and walked over to the door to let Papa in.

"Sir, we have something to tell you."

"Oh my, I hope it isn't bad news."

"No Papa, it is the best news ever. I am going to have a baby."

He ran over to hug me. "Oh Asphodel, you have made me a happy and wealthy man. The wealth of having another grandchild to love!" Pride in his last words shown on him like the sun beaming on the most beautiful flower in the garden. We were truly blessed beyond all measure.

Chapter 37

The next few months went by so quickly I almost did not mind the morning sickness and the fatigue. Once Dr. Haynes made it official, it seemed as though I grew like a weed. Benjamin was always concerned I was doing too much, but I promised him I would take lots of rest breaks each day.

Our summer for 1873 was one of the driest summers on record. My poor asphodels were suffering, but they were still blooming, just at a snail's pace. It was late July, but this morning, it was not so humid out. Benjamin and Papa had gone into town early to buy lumber. So, I decided it would be nice to go sit on my cemetery bench before the sun came up with a vengeance. As I walked outside, I could see someone sitting on my bench. I thought to myself, this was unusual. Who might it be?

As I moved closer, I saw that it was Berenice. Oh, how I have missed her. I could not wait to tell her the news. "Berenice, how nice to see you."

"Asphodel, what a lovely surprise! I thought I would stop for a spell. I am so sorry I have not been around to see you. I have been away too long when I should have come sooner." She said sullenly.

"Berenice, are you all right? You seem to be suffering from melancholy."

"Oh Asphodel, I have been under the weather, so to speak of late, but it comes and goes."

As I looked at her now that I was seated beside her, she did look a little paler than usual. "I am sorry you have been ill. I hope this fresh air will make you feel a little better. I am sure you can see, it is no secret, but

165

I am with child. Benjamin and I are over the moon with excitement. The baby will be here sometime in October."

"I am so happy for the both of you and your family."

"Thank you, Berenice."

We sat there just staring out at the headstones and the asphodels admiring the simplistic beauty on this lovely summer morning. Before I knew it, she was gone. She would vanish into thin air every now and then. I decided to keep sitting because I knew Benjamin would not want me walking around too much. I even decided to prop up my feet on the bench as I laid on my side next to the tree that always provided a canopy from the sun. I felt perfectly bliss, knowing my child would be here in just a few short months as I became sleepy. I yawned with my eyes heavy as lead. I saw a man walking outside the fence striking a match to light his cigar as I dozed off with not a care in the world.

Chapter 38

I began to stir because I felt warm. It was going to be a hot day after all. Who knew how long I stayed asleep. In a groggy state with my eyes still closed, I began hearing my name, and the air seemed to become almost hot, not humid, just hot. Again, I heard my name louder than before. It was Astra. My eyes began to blink into reality where all I saw was brightness. Lots of it all around me. In the distance, I could see Astra running towards me in what looked like flames all around her. Was I dreaming? Startled, I sat up to find the entire cemetery was on fire and I was in the middle of it. The smoke began taking hold of my lungs like a strangler putting his hands on my neck. I saw Astra trying to find a way to me as she had to stop, coughing at every movement, trying to shield herself with her shawl.

She reached me finally, but I did not realize how much the smoke was affecting my lungs and I was having a hard time moving as quickly as she wanted me to. "Asphodel, lean on me and I will get you out of here. Be brave."

We started moving a little faster and all I heard was her continuing to cough as she held the shawl trying to protect me from the fumes. I was in such a daze, and it happened so fast, all I remember was both of us falling down on the ground close to the house, Astra's shawl still wrapped around my head. I was able to squint ever so slightly to see Astra unmoving with tattered charred clothing and her face covered in black soot. I reached out my hand to her, clasping it with mine as my eyes closed and I drifted away.

"Asphodel, darling!"

I heard my name again, but this time, it was a man's voice. However, it was not just any man; it was my beloved Benjamin. I stirred, coming to, feeling extremely tired, weak, and almost unable to breathe.

"Darling."

"Benjamin, give her time. Let her ease back into waking up."

I continued to stir wondering what was going on, my mind racing. "Ben…Benjamin. Are you there?"

"Yes, Asphodel." He seemed incredibly anxious and upset, and I could not figure out why.

"What time is it? Why are you calling me so?"

"Asphodel, this is Dr. Haynes, try to slowly open your eyes."

The doctor, what was he doing here. I tried to follow along with his directions, but I was having a hard time. "I'm trying Dr."

"Take your time. Do not force yourself."

I knew I was lying down, and then it came to me—the baby. I suddenly became overwrought with horror. I jolted upright, widely opening my eyes, clutching my belly so tight, and screaming, "My baby! Is there something wrong with my baby?!"

Benjamin closed his hand around mine as Dr. Haynes interjected, "Asphodel, settle down. You have been through an awful ordeal, which you may not have any memory of right at the moment, but I can tell you one absolute—your baby is perfectly healthy."

A sigh of relief settled in as Benjamin embraced me closely as I reciprocated back to him. "Dr., then what happened?" I uttered, coughing harshly.

My father stepped in and came by the other side of the bed, "Daughter, a few mornings ago, when Benjamin and I had gone into town for lumber, you must have wandered out into the cemetery. You know how dry it has been these past few months. Well, something caught the grass on fire in the cemetery while you were in it. By the grace of God, you are still alive."

"Yes, and you are going to need your rest because you breathed in quite a bit of that smoke and your lungs need time to recover from it." Dr. Haynes added.

"How long have I been asleep?"

"Three days. We thought we were going to lose you." Dr. Haynes said emphatically.

"Oh, my goodness. How…?" I quizzed as Dr. Haynes waved at Benjamin and Papa to leave the room. Something seemed amiss, but I was too weak to fight for the answers now.

"Darling, you need your rest. We will talk later when you are feeling a little better." Benjamin said as he kissed my forehead, floating his hand across my cheek, his warmth tingling my senses.

"But Benjamin, how did I get out of the cemetery alive?"

"Astra saved you."

Before I could say or ask anything else, he quietly shut the door behind him.

Chapter 39

I woke up to a new day with the doctor ready to give me some medicine. It tasted icky, but I took it. I could not believe what had happened, but I was so grateful I was alive and so was my unborn child. What of Astra though? No one would tell me. "Dr. Haynes, please tell me, how is my sister? Did she die in that fire? Is that why no one wants to tell me?"

"Asphodel, remain calm and I will tell you what happened. To ease your nerves, Astra is still with us, but very sick. She has not woken up since Winnie found the two of you laid out on the grass just outside the back door. As soon as Winnie knew you two were out of the fire's reach, she sent Johnny into town to quickly get the Metzengerstein Fire Brigade and me.

I road back with Johnny in the carriage as the fire brigade beat us to the house. When Johnny and I arrived, we immediately ran to the two of you, carrying you into the house, away from all the smoke and any lingering danger. You were both unconscious, but I did all I could do until Benjamin and your father returned home to help me move you two up to your rooms. I sent Johnny to find them. As luck would have it, they were already heading back to the house as Johnny ran into them on the road. They moved quickly into the house, where we carefully moved the two of you to your rooms as Winnie helped with your burnt and smoky dresses. Thank heavens Astra moved you out of the cemetery as fast as she did. Your high-necked dress assisted in saving your life keeping the fire away from burning your skin.

So, now you have it—all the details of that terrible day—are you satisfied now?"

"Thank you Dr. Haynes. I just had to know what happened."

"Child, I cannot tell you how scared I was at the thought of losing you and your sister. I delivered you both into the world. You are the twinkle in your father's eyes. Don't tell him I said this, but he is like a child when he speaks to me of that grandbaby arriving in just a few months. Also, he goes on about Astra's little darling, Dahlia, all the time. You girls have made him the happiest man alive."

"Oh Dahlia! Is she okay? Do please tell me about Astra. How is she?" Asking uncontrollably able to contain myself at the thought of both Astra and Dahlia.

"Asphodel, I am with her a great deal, doing everything I can for her. You must rest, and then we will talk more." He insisted.

"May Benjamin come in?"

"Of course, I'll go fetch him."

Just like that, Dr. Haynes kept Astra's condition a secret, challenging me to worry more than I already had been. I hope Benjamin will not keep me in the dark.

Within fifteen minutes, Benjamin entered the room, smiling sheepishly at me. I could assume because he felt like he was not helping enough, but I knew deep in my soul he was doing everything he had the power to do. He walked over to me with a tip toed gate as if I was asleep. I perked up at the sight of his beautiful face and twinkling eyes as he gazed upon mine. I easily scooted over in the bed, patting it with my hand softly as a signal for him to sit down.

As Benjamin sat on the side of the bed, holding my hand, we smiled longingly at one another both of us thinking about the same thing: Astra.

"Benjamin, has the doctor said anything hopeful?"

"He hasn't said anything positive or negative. We just have to wait."

"It is exacerbating – the waiting."

"I know, but Dr. Haynes is monitoring her closely. Winnie has been taking care of Dahlia."

"Oh my, could you have Winnie bring Dahlia to me for a visit, please?"

"Darling, you need your strength, and you are still utterly weak." Benjamin emphasized.

"Please, Benjamin! If I could just visit with her for a short while…"

"I will ask Dr. Haynes. If he deems it suitable, I will have Winnie bring her in."

The bedroom door opened with an inexcusable force as Papa ran in, outwardly out of breath. "Benjamin…Asphodel…come quickly…Astra is waking up!"

"Oh, Papa!"

"Asphodel…she is asking for you."

Chapter 40

I lifted myself from the waist up too quickly as the blood rushed to my head, but I wanted to be there for my sister. I fell back against my pillows as Benjamin urged, "Darling, easy now, as Dr. Haynes, your father, and I have continually reminded you over and over—you are weak. Do not move."

As he was saying this, he stood up and scooped me up into his arms and carried me out of our bedroom, through the hallway, and into Astra's room without hesitation. My father had already placed a chair by Astra's bedside for me to sit directly beside her. Benjamin placed me in the chair gently.

No one prepared me for the effects of the fire on my sister. She was my mirror image; however, now, she was bandaged it seemed from head to toe. Much of her face wore white gauze as if she was mummified, but I could see her eyes and her lips. She had on a very light nightgown, but I could see the bandages underneath and around her arms with her left hand completely covered. Her right hand was the only part of her open and free to the air like a bird. Unfortunately, that bird could not fly away to freedom as her hand did have a few marks from the fire weighing her down.

I looked at Dr. Haynes with tears beginning to pool in my eyes, reaching for her hand quietly asking for his approval upon my reaction. He nodded his head with a slight smile, but his eyes told more of the story than his smile—Astra woke up, but for how long.

"Astra, it is Asphodel. I am here and ever so grateful to you for saving my life."

"Aspho…del. Are you…alright? The…baby?" Astra articulated as best as she could.

"Astra, please do not speak too much. You need your strength right now." Dr. Haynes interjected authoritatively.

"Doctor," Astra paused to cough, "I need…Asphodel…alone," eeking out words one by one in between fits of coughing.

Not only were Dr. Haynes and I in the room, but Papa and Benjamin were also there. Her request to be alone with me was not taken approvingly with the men in the room to easily honor her request. "Astra, you woke up only minutes ago. I need…" Dr. Haynes tried to explain, but Papa interrupted this time.

"I think we should let the two of them talk for a few minutes. We can be right outside the door if either of them needs us." Papa suggested.

"Thomas, I…"

Papa put up a hand, "Miles," as he took that same hand and offered him the way to the door. Papa and Benjamin followed behind, not before Benjamin kissed the top of my head on the way out. Benjamin eased the door shut, giving us privacy.

An uncomfortable feeling lingered in the room as a prodigal son showing up at Christmas dinner. Astra should save her strength, so I broke the ice between us. "Astra, I owe you and my baby our lives. If you had not seen us, we would have perished in the fire. Thank you. I am so sorry we have been fighting all these years. I love you and I need you as not only my sister, but as my friend."

Struggling to speak, "I love you… Asphodel. Please listen to me," she said so quietly I could hardly hear her. I leaned in closer. "I need you to take care of Dahlia for me. Raise her as your own."

"Astra, you will be here for her."

"Asphodel, keep her safe…from Alfred. I am so sorry for how I treated you our whole lives. You are my dear sister, and you will be a wonderful mother."

"Astra, what are you saying?"

"Mother, hold on. I'll be there soon."

"No, you can't leave me! Not now! Benjamin, Papa!" I screamed as the three men rushed in the room.

"Papa, I love you, but Mother is calling for me." Astra said staring up at the ceiling.

"Astra, I love you so, my first born…" Papa stopped because he was filled with uncontrollable tears flooding his eyes, standing in disbelief at what was about to happen.

"Goodbye, Asphodel…Papa…Benjamin. Tell Dahlia I will always love her."

At that moment, Astra breathed her last breath as Dr. Haynes checked her pulse and tenderly closed her eyes. Everyone in the room was crying profusely from the death of this young, vibrant woman, gone too soon, even with her haughty disposition and loose morals—Astra was family.

Benjamin carried me back to our room at the doctor's request while he walked Papa down the stairs for a brandy. Once I was settled into bed, I told Benjamin what Astra said to me. At his astonishment, "Dear, what about Alfred? Dahlia is his daughter."

"Before the fire, I confronted Astra about her visit because I had a feeling about her relationship with Alfred. He loved the excitement of the two of them; nonetheless, three were too many, so he told Astra to leave and take the baby, never to return. No one knows this but us. I promised her to keep these secrets, but I feel you must know this information."

"What a pale comparison of a man Alfred is! Regardless of what Astra did to me and us, he has no right to do that to an innocent child."

"I agree. Because Papa can not know about this, we will have to contact Alfred about Astra's death. If he even shows up for her funeral, you and I will confront him about Dahlia. If my intuition is correct, I believe he will pay his respects and high tail it out of here without one thought of that precious girl."

Chapter 41

Papa was taking this so hard, rightfully so, Benjamin handled all of the funeral arrangements. Dr. Haynes still had me on bed rest; otherwise, I would have helped Benjamin. The only task he would let me take care of was the letter to Alfred about Astra's death. We did not want to take a chance on the mail system not getting the letter there promptly, so Johnny went on horseback to Alfred's home, passing the letter onto Alfred and Alfred only. Johnny was instructed to bring a response back with him. Benjamin gave Johnny enough money to stay at an inn overnight and return the next day.

Around seven o'clock in the morning, we were sitting at the kitchen table for breakfast as Winnie was placing biscuits, jam, and sausage for us. Dr. Haynes allowed me to begin coming downstairs for meals to help bring my strength back, so I was very happy when we heard footsteps coming up the back walkway, bringing in Johnny with a response from Alfred.

"Oh, Johnny, I am ever so gleeful you have returned. Please, sit down for breakfast. You must have left before sunrise to get home."

"Yes ma'am, I did. I knew you would be needing Mr. Griswold's answer."

"Benjamin, what did he say?"

"He will be here on Monday, the day of the funeral. I will share the rest with you after breakfast." Benjamin surreptitiously replied.

We ate and spoke with Johnny about Alfred's demeanor when he met him, Alfred's house, and his trip in general. Once we were finished, Benjamin assisted me upstairs to lie back down where he would tell me the rest of what Alfred said in the letter.

"Well, I guess I will just read the letter aloud.

To Mr. Richardson,

Thank you for quickly notifying me of Astra's passing and the funeral details you and the Willoughby family have set forth for her. Having already made the decision to bury her in the Willoughby family plot, I agree with this decision. I will come into town on Monday morning for the funeral, but will not be staying any longer than the services take. Please have the child and her things ready for me upon departure after the funeral.

Sincerely,

Mr. Alfred R. Griswold

"Oh, Benjamin, what a cold-hearted man!"

"I know. It is going to be rather difficult being around him at all next Monday."

"How he mentions Dahlia is almost sinful for a father to refer to his own flesh and blood. What are we going to do? We cannot let him take her."

"You said Astra insisted you and I raise Dahlia, so I think we need to be ready with legalities for Mr. Griswold when he is ready to depart after Astra's funeral. I will take care of everything darling. Please do not worry and please get some rest. The next few days are going to be quite stressful for you."

"Yes, Benjamin." I could not stop crying, still in disbelief Astra was gone.

He came over to me and hugged me with such comfort and confidence, I knew I had no fears about what was to come. He stared at me for a moment, leaning in for a tumultuous kiss I was not expecting, embracing me now. He looked up at me again, still holding me, and commanded, "Asphodel, you know our little bundle will be here in less than three months and we have no names chosen. We need to make some choices."

I beamed because of two things: he was right and he was taking my mind off of Astra. He wanted me not to worry. "I will work on a list of boys' and girls' names, but you must do the same."

"Yes, ma'am, I will. You know though, why would we pick out girls' names, Richardsons always have boys," he sarcastically sneered.

Chapter 42

Stuck inside the house for around two weeks was not my normal practice, but everyone was treating me like a porcelain doll because of the fire, Astra's death, and my unborn child. I woke up rather early the day before Astra's funeral. I still could not believe my sister was gone; furthermore, she saved my life. A girl so selfish her entire life and despising me only to be incredibly unselfish at the end. Even though we were not on pleasant terms, I knew I would always love my sister, and we would eventually patch our relationship given time. Now, time is *nevermore* for us.

Dawn was slightly arriving like an old friend with a candle being lit as I decided to look out the window. I had forgotten how the twilight time of the morning before the dawn arose with a splendid sunrise provided such peace. I stood there with the curtain parted, holding it back as my right arm held my lace shawl around my shoulders, giving me enough warmth to feel comfort. The window I peered through showed me the view of the front yard, green as ever the eye could see. Soon, fall would arrive, sweeping away the green for brown with a coolness before winter. I could not wait because in this time, my child would arrive to greet me and Benjamin.

I carefully moved to the side window, for which I had been told to ignore because of the damage caused by the fire. Since I was alone, I decided I must see the cemetery before tomorrow. I could not bear the thought of seeing the devastation of the grounds and watching my sister interred all in one moment. I put my hand on the curtain and paused, looking down and looking for strength. In that pause, I felt a hand over

179

mine on the curtain and another hand around my waist as my back became warm with the closeness of the man I loved. Benjamin had stealthily entered the parlor to greet me. I felt him bend down a little to caress my face with his as he kissed my cheek, running his lips down the side of my neck, resting them on my shoulder, kissing me there like a whisper on my skin as my whole body tingled with goosebumps at the delight of his touch.

"Asphodel, you know you should not be down here, especially standing, by yourself. What if you had fainted and hurt yourself?"

"Benjamin, I feel fine. I was restless and could not sleep, so I snuck down here to look outside and enjoy the sunrise."

"You should have awakened me. I am so happy I woke up, so now we can revel in the sunrise together," he paused because I had a sullen look on my face, "What is wrong? I can tell you are not telling me everything."

"You and Papa have kept me from seeing the cemetery grounds. I need to see how bad they look before tomorrow. I cannot endure the thought of seeing both the grounds and Astra's funeral all in the same day. Please let me look! Even better, please take me outside to see it."

Benjamin, silent in his thoughts, studying me closely before giving his answer, "It is quite difficult saying no to you."

I smiled, reaching up to kiss him, "Thank you."

He took my hand and we walked to the kitchen where Winnie was beginning to make breakfast. We greeted her and moved to the back door. Benjamin paused with his hand on the door handle, "Asphodel, I need to prepare you for this. It looks bleak because it is. The tombstones are blackened with soot and ash and the ground…is even more horrible than you can ever imagine. We will bring it back to its glory, but it will take a great deal of time. Are you ready?"

"Yes, I am."

He opened the door and put his arm through mine, escorting me outside. The sunrise was imminent, where a hint of light was coming over the cemetery with the break of dawn. We slowly walked over to the tombstones closest to the house. On the ground, it was like a division of black and green coating the ground where grass used to thrive. All the tombstones affected by the fire were blackened, just as Benjamin said. The cruelest sight of all were the asphodels—they were gone. The cemetery appeared as if no one had taken care of it for a thousand years. The devastation overwhelmed me as Benjamin thought it would. I doubled over, sobbing for my namesake as if they were my children. He caught me as I almost fell to the ground.

"Asphodel, we will bring them back. I promise with every ounce of strength I will." He clutched me in his arms, pressing his body so close to mine, I could hardly breathe. He let me bawl blubberingly as if I was a child who lost her favorite toy. We stood there in this somber embrace for what seemed an eternity. I felt and saw the sun rise upon us. At first, it seemed like the sun was punishing me for bringing more light for me to witness the fire's aftermath, but then I thought of what Benjamin just said and I knew the sun was a beacon of hope of what was to come for our lives, the cemetery, and my asphodels.

Chapter 43

The next morning arrived as fast as a falcon flying to feed on its prey. Everything was ready in the parlor, and Astra was breathtaking underneath her shroud. Even as a corpse, she would be the most beautiful woman in the room. Many townspeople arrived for the funeral, including our dressmaker, Madame White; our printer, Mr. Meredith, the baker, and the newspaper editor. Benjamin's mother arrived and hugged me tightly as a mother would. I was so thankful for Lenore. She was not only such a guiding presence throughout this awful ordeal, but she had been a gem throughout my pregnancy.

The minister was ready and so we all sat down in the front row of chairs. "Family and friends, we gather today to pay our respects to a young lady taken too soon—a hero at the very end—Astra Daffodil Willoughby Griswold. *Yea, though I walk through the valley of the shadow of death, I will fear no evil: for thou art with me; thy rod and thy staff they comfort me.*"

As the minister spoke her name and quoted from the Bible, I took Papa's hand and held it tight. I stayed strong for him, but I was pure mush inside. I never thought of life without my twin. Now, I had no mother, and no sister. I felt alone. All I could think of was part of Edgar Allan Poe's poem, *Alone*:

From childhood's hour I have not been
As others were — I have not seen
As others saw — I could not bring

My passions from a common spring —
From the same source I have not taken
My sorrow — I could not awaken
My heart to joy at the same tone —
And all I lov'd — I lov'd alone —

But I was not alone! My mind was in wind tunnel moving my thoughts around in a cyclone. I could not focus on the minister because my heart hurt so. A touch of a hand woke me from my daymare of utter loss from chaos stemming from the two females who should be here with me for the birth of my first child. The warmth from Benjamin's hand soothed me as I beamed up at him, realizing my pity party must end right now. Coming back to reality, I heard the minister finish:

"Thy soul shall find itself alone,
Mid dark thoughts of the grey tombstone —
Not one, of all the crowd to pry
Into thine hour of secrecy —
Be silent in thy solitude
Which is not loneliness — for then
The spirits of the dead who stood
In life before thee are again
In death around thee, and their will
Shall then oershadow thee — be still."

On the last line of the poem he read, I looked up with mournful eyes, and I swear I saw Astra walking away hand in hand with a woman. The sight happened so fast, I blinked, and they were gone. Could it have been my mother escorting Astra away? Oh no, I must be hallucinating. In that moment, I also realized no man introduced himself to us as Mr. Alfred Griswold. Surely, he was here; but then again, what if he was that spiteful not to attend his own wife's funeral?

We walked out to the cemetery where our family plots lie in wait, all except for Astra now. The August day was bright and beautiful as my sister. No clouds darkened this day, just the blackness of the ground and tombstones all around us added a level of severe sadness. However, the deep purple flowers, her namesake, dominated her casket like a crown all fitting for my sister. Asters do not have a scent, but the leaves do. Oh, how fragrant they are when a little crushed. Today, some were, so there was an aroma of a balsam like mint spilling into the air. Papa, Benjamin, and I took one flower from her coffin. As her casket was lowered into the ground with the minister adding more sentiments and praying, we threw our flowers into her grave along with a handful of dirt.

We remained outside for a while as the mourners paid their respects to us. Winnie had brought a chair outside for me to sit in, knowing I still needed to keep up my energy. Some family friends were walking away when I heard my name as a question, "Asphodel?" I turned to look and saw a man walking up to me. He was dressed in black with his crepe on his hat. He was tall with a strong build, had well-combed brown hair with long brown sideburns, and small brown eyes peering at me as if he knew me. I studied him for a moment and realized this had to be none other than, "Alfred?"

"Yes, Asphodel. I only knew it was you because you are the spitting image of your sister. The funeral was absolutely beautiful. I could not have planned anything more appropriate for her."

"Thank you, Alfred," I grabbed Benjamin's hand so he would turn around, "This is my husband, Benjamin Richardson."

They shook each other's hands and gave pleasantries, but Benjamin had to keep his cool, knowing the truth about how Alfred treated Astra. My father turned towards us, and I repeated the same introductions.

"Sir, I regret this is how we are meeting for the first time."

"Mr. Griswold, I do agree, but if it had not been for Astra, Asphodel would have perished. There is nothing positive that came out of the fire. How long might you be staying? I can have a room ready for you to stay with us." Papa responded mannerly, but with no feeling at all.

"I sent a letter ahead of time to let you know I would be here only for the funeral, but I would not be lodging overnight. I instructed for Dahlia to be packed with her things ready for me to take her home."

"My husband and I read your letter, but we did not tell my father. Papa, I am sorry we kept Mr. Griswold's attendance today from you, but you did not need one more thing to worry over."

"Asphodel, it would have been fine telling me. What I do not think fine is you are taking my granddaughter out of this house while her mother is hardly placed in the dirt. I do apologize for my uncouth language, but you will not remove her tonight."

"Sir, I am the child's father, and her place is with me." Griswold insisted.

"Have you arranged for a nursemaid for Dahlia?" I interrupted.

"Uh, no, not yet, but Astra's lady's maid is still working at my house, and she volunteered to look after the child until I am able to find an acceptable nursemaid."

"Thomas, I think it better to move into your study away from the few mourners who are left so they do not eavesdrop on our conversation." Benjamin suggested.

"Thank you, Benjamin. Mr. Griswold, please come this way."

We moved into the house and into my father's study where a gentleman was waiting. "Mr. Enoch, this is my father-in law, Mr. Thomas Willoughby, my brother-in-law, Mr. Alfred Griswold, and my wife, Mrs. Asphodel Richardson. Everyone, please take a seat here," Benjamin instructed as he put a hand out toward the chairs sitting around my father's desk.

"I say, what is this all about? Who are you?" Alfred demanded, looking at Mr. Enoch.

"Mr. Griswold, I am an attorney. Mr. Richardson asked me to come here to discuss the matter of a child, Dahlia," he said as he looked at a document with his spectacles. "On Mrs. Griswold's death bed, she instructed Mrs. Richardson for Dahlia to be raised by her and her husband. She highly insisted for you to dissolve your rights from the child and sign them over to her sister, basically allowing them to adopt the child."

Standing up with fervor, "I will not stand for this nonsense. That child is mine and she will leave with me. What proof is there Astra requested this?"

"You have my word!"

"Your word is worth nothing if no one else heard it."

"Mr. Griswold, Asphodel has never lied in her life, and that is a true fact. You will not insult her." My father stated firmly.

"Mr. Griswold, why do you want Dahlia back? Astra told Asphodel a great deal of information about your relationship that might not look too well on you." Benjamin offered.

"Alfred, did you send my sister away with Dahlia?" I asked hesitatingly.

"I think she misunderstood my intentions. I would never turn away from my own child."

"You did not answer my question, nor my husband's."

Everyone in the room stared at Alfred until he grimaced, placing his head in his hands and wincing his hair. "I loved Astra, but I did not want any children. She knew this, and she still did what she wanted."

"You despicable human being! I am so happy Astra came to us, but I wished she had shared this with me. You basically abandoned the both of them!" Papa yelled.

"But I didn't! I told her I would give her money for her and the child."

"Alfred, Astra loved you and you turned her away. Please allow us to adopt Dahlia. She will receive everything she needs from us—love, shelter, etc."

"I can give her those things as well."

Benjamin interrupted, "You may provide for her financially, but you will not give her the love we can. You kicked out your own wife and child."

"I could grow to love the child. No one knows I sent Astra and the child away except you, so those are your words against mine."

"Mathematics plays a striking hand in this game you are playing, Mr. Griswold."

"Whatever do you mean, Mr. Richardson?"

"Astra disclosed to my wife she was with child before your nuptials. I think our quaint town of Spencerton would most certainly spread this story around like wildfire; don't you?"

"These citizens might thrive on the gossip, but it is just one little town. Besides, you have no proof!"

"There are matters of a marriage license and a birth certificate. Mr. Enoch?"

Mr. Enoch followed Benjamin's suggestion and pulled the two pieces of paper out on the desk for Alfred to peruse. Alfred looked upon the documents as if he was the cat who ate the canary. His shoulders drooped with defeat and his face grew pale almost with a gray hue about him. His pallor began to take on the tone of someone who was sick to his stomach. He turned his weathered eyes up to Mr. Enoch, considering the matter, and then looked back down at the papers as he balled his fists up like a top wound up too tightly. He slowly turned back to Benjamin, now with his hollowed eyes burning like two embers in a fire.

Benjamin remained calm, watching his eyes as to what Alfred would do next. "Mr. Griswold, may I remind you, if you plan on striking at me, I will have you thrown in jail for assault."

As Benjamin finished his statement, Alfred freed his hands from his own tightness, relaxed his shoulders and merely fell down in a chair, slumping and placing his hand over his face. Remaining in this position for several minutes, no one in the room made a sound. By the way he was acting, it was evident he knew he was beaten. The one attribute I knew about this man was what I inferred from what Astra always told me about him—appearances and his reputation meant everything to him above all else. It was one thing for him to take my sister to places where they were unknown doing unspeakable acts; moreover, he could get away with people knowing. However, to have the proof of Dahlia's conception thrown to the citizens of Spencerton, and maybe even Richmond, he could never allow it to occur. Now, some may think Alfred a Casanova, but for everyone to know Alfred was a scoundrel, he would be ruined as a person and a businessman. Additionally, he would bring wretchedness on his family name.

It seemed we waited for eternity for him to look up, but he finally brought his hand down and placed both hands upon his knees, standing up cooly, only looking at Mr. Enoch.

"Mr. Enoch, where do I sign?"

As he said this, Benjamin and I looked at each other with a fullness in our hearts. Astra saved my life, and now we were saving Dahlia's. Mr. Enoch had Benjamin sign the paperwork and then Griswold was gone, out of our lives, hopefully for good.

"Thank you, Mr. Enoch." Benjamiin said as he shook his hand.

"You are welcome. I thought we might have had a true fight on our hands for a few moments."

I added with a smile, "He knew what the right thing was to do. Scandal was not in Alfred's vocabulary. As soon as he gave up on Astra and Dahlia when he told my sister to leave his house, he knew allowing us to raise Dahlia as ours would be what Astra wanted in the end."

Chapter 44

The next two months went by slowly as the waiting seemed so long as I grew much larger. Still, I remained in a surrealistic state of mind reminding myself everyday Astra was gone. Even with our constant bickering, I had no idea how I was going to endure the rest of my life without her. Dahlia was a blessing to keep me grounded. Every time I looked at her, I saw my sister in her eyes. Being her mother now enriched me with such a special gift. She was adjusting, and I am sure with me, the spitting image of her mother, gave her help. Nonetheless, she was so young, she truly did not understand. In the long run, this would help her I knew deep in my heart.

The evening of October 26th, I went to bed early, feeling a bit uneasy, unsure what I did not exactly know. I attributed it to knowing the baby would be coming soon. As I slept and lay there off and on all night, I was restless. I decided to walk around, and trying not to wake up Benjamin was a feat unto itself. He had become such a light sleeper since my pregnancy began. Unbelievably, I was able to tip toe out of the room quietly enough, I did not wake him. I wanted to go outside, but I knew Benjamin and Papa would have my hide if I did, so I decided to walk around downstairs. I entered the hallway and realized I had not brought a candle with me, but I knew this house as if it was an old friend guiding me every day up and down the stairs, so my hesitation evaporated into the air like a well-performed chemical reaction. I held onto the railing and began my descent. As I slowly stepped, I suddenly saw someone downstairs who seemed familiar. It startled me because it was a man—not Papa, not Benjamin, and not Johnny. Wobbling with a slight fear, I clung to the rail, only to catch myself before I slipped.

189

Making it down the stairs with my heart racing, I went into the parlor where it seemed this person went. When I entered the room, he was there. He seemed so recognizable, asking myself where I had seen him before. I paused, thinking, unsettled to speak to him. I was frozen, but not fearful. Who was he? Flashes of memories sorted through my mind like a photo album filled with pictures. Wait! He was the man for whom I saw in the cemetery more than once! "Sir, who are you? I have seen you before, but I have no idea what your name is? How did you get in this house?"

"Asphodel, we met in the cemetery—a few times, but I never introduced myself. I am Mr. Richardson."

"Mr. Richardson? How are you related to Benjamin and Lenore?"

"In life, I was Lenore's husband and Benjamin was my adopted son."

At the moment Mr. Richardson said "was," a flood of emotion swept through my entire body pooling sweat on my forehead; furthermore, I realized a large pool of water was on the floor. Trying to race for a chair, I fell on my bottom, crying out in pain. Mr. Richardson spoke, "Dear Asphodel, you are the angel my son deserved, and I am so proud of how you and he love each other endlessly. I have been watching over you and Benjamin. I know it is time to move on because you do not need me anymore. I wish I could be here to see my grandchildren grow up. Precious Asphodel, I will see you again." As he spoke and I was taking it all in, I screamed again, hurting so. I only turned my head once, and then he was gone. I must be hallucinating from the pain, or having a horrible night terror.

What was I to do, my screams were unheard. The pain crept up on me again as if vines were strangling my insides where I let out a shriek hopefully waking the dead. I tried to control my anxiety from being alone, but then I heard noises from upstairs followed by running footsteps down the stairs. Benjamin arrived in lightning speed. "Darling, what happened? I told you to wake me, if…" He saw the water on the floor and stopped. He ran to get my father, who sent Johnny to get the doctor, and came back, scooping me up in his arms, bringing me back to our bed. Once I opened my eyes, I saw Papa and Winnie right behind Benjamin. All at once, I felt fear, anxiety, and love in the room. My baby was about to be born.

Once Dr. Haynes arrived, he sent everyone out of the room. He brought a nurse with him to assist. "Asphodel, you and the baby are going to be fine. Just relax and listen to me when I tell you what to do."

"Yes, Dr. Haynes."

When I went downstairs, I knew the time was somewhere around three o'clock in the morning, so it must be about an hour later now. I had no idea what to expect. Oh, how I wish my mother was here, or Astra. I had to do this alone and without either of them. Pain was causing me to doubt myself, but I kept hearing Dr. Haynes and the nurse encouraging me and giving me directions.

I labored for an extremely long time because the sun rose, shining through the window as a beacon of hope. The pain became stronger as Dr. Haynes instructed me. Before I knew it, I heard a little cry. I did it, my baby was here!

"Asphodel, it is a boy!"

I cried uncontrollably with joyful tears running down my face. The nurse was cleaning him up when I told Dr. Haynes thank you. "Please get Benjamin!"

"In just a moment, my dear." Dr. Haynes elated proudly of seeing my happy face.

As the nurse was bringing the baby over to me, I had another pain and I let out a yelp. Then another pain came faster than the ones before. "Dr. Haynes, what is wrong?"

He ran over to me, checking for anything wrong, as I continued to wince in agony. It seemed he was taking way too long and began to panic.

Thoughts of knowing my mother died during childbirth running through my mind.

"Asphodel, I do not know how to tell you this…"

I cut him off, "What is it?!"

"You are having twins! So, let's do what we just did one more time."

This time, the second baby came more easily, but my strength was gone. I heard the baby cry and then I was in a daze, almost as if I passed out, lingering along. Where was I? I could make out the audible sounds of Dr. Haynes and the nurse, but what were they saying? I began to hear words: babies…blood…fear. I could feel my heart beating faster, and then slower, and slower, to the point I felt numb. My mind was swimming with thoughts and pictures as I grew cold. All I wanted to do was go to sleep. The room seemed to grow darker as well. I felt number…and then…nothing.

Chapter 46

"I did not know about the second baby. Whenever I did checkups with Asphodel, I only heard one heartbeat. Once she started having more flare-ups after the first baby was born, I quickly checked and there was a second heartbeat, but there was also more blood than there should have been. The second baby boy was born and then she simply gave out, her pulse weakening with every minute." Dr. Haynes explained to Benjamin.

"What happens now?" Tears rolled into Benjamin's eyes as he asked.

"Come into the room, please." The door was open, but Benjamin and Dr. Haynes were talking right outside in the hallway. They entered the room as I had woken up and the nurse had given me both boys, one in each arm, to welcome their father to see us.

"Darling, oh how blessed we are! They are beautiful!"

"I know. I still cannot believe twins."

"Dr. Haynes told me about the scare you gave him. He thought he lost you."

"I had too much to fight for." I gleefully stated, looking at the two boys.

As Benjamin took one of the boys and held him, I thought about the crazy dream I had about his father coming to see me. It did not dawn on me as he said it, but now, I should have known I was having twins because he said grandchildren. I chuckled at that thought. If I told Benjamin and Dr. Haynes, they would send me to a sanitorium.

"You know, we never did finalize a name, let alone two. What should we name them?"

"Well, my darling wife, one should be named Robert because that is the one boy's name we settled upon. Thoughts on a second name?"

"I think Edward, but I also have thoughts on their middle names."

"And?."

"I think we should give them their grandfathers' names as their middles names: Robert Thomas and Edward Guy."

Benjamin regarded me, stroking his hand over his chin contemplating my suggestion for a few moments, "I think those are perfect names for our boys. I love you, Asphodel!"

"I love you too, Benjamin."

We kissed while each of us held our welcome additions to our family. Life could not get any better than this exact instant.

Chapter 47

After a few months, Benjamin and I began to restore the cemetery back to its original glory. We scrubbed the blackness from the tombstones the rain had not washed away. We planted new grass seeds to restore the lawn. Unfortunately, the asphodels did not appear. I was afraid they were gone forever.

The next few years, our little family thrived as the children grew older as they learned to crawl, talk, and walk becoming their own little personalities. The family business also continued to thrive. My father and Benjamin always staying abreast of new techniques and procedures in the funeral industry. My father even changed the name to Willoughby and Son. Benjamin grinned from ear to ear the day the new placard went up.

In the blink of an eye, it was time for the children to attend school. They were so excited for this new learning adventure. Dahlia was six and Robert and Edward were 5. Even though Dahlia was not quite a year older than the twins, she bossed them around, but they would not have it any other way.

At the end of one of their school days late in September, they came rushing in through the cemetery where I was weeding close to our own family plot. "Mother, mother, school was so much fun today. Our teacher read to us *Alice's Adventures in Wonderland* by Lewis Carroll. Even Robert and Edward actually paid attention." Dahlia reported.

"Dahlia, we love to be read to as Mother and Father always do at bedtime." Robert interjected.

Edward added, "But we also studied mathematics, which I like better."

"Children, I am so happy you did well with your schooling today. Why don't you go inside and put on your play clothes and come back out and keep me company?"

They all agreed, zooming into the house like a swarm of bees. They would attack Winnie upon entry, but this was an attack she was used to. I kept working, moving along from grave to grave when the children came back out changed into clothes, which did not matter if they became dirty.

Always dutiful Dahlia asked, "Mother, may we help?"

"Of course, darling. Boys come over here with us and let me show you what you are looking for as you help me." I showed them the types of weeds I was pulling up. "Now, if you see anything else, call for me to come see it. We do not want to pull up any types of flowers, especially the ones I showed you in the book the other day."

"You mean the asphodels." Edward reminded me.

"Yes, the asphodels."

We all went to work, the children scattered about. Dahlia and Edward were very serious about weeding with Robert pulling weeds, but also mesmerized by any insects he found.

"Mother, mother, come over here. I think I found something different." Dahlia yelled, inviting me to have a look.

I asked her to stand up because I could not see her for the tombstones. As she jumped up, I saw she was in our family plot, which took me a little aback, but I proceeded to where she was. "Sweetheart, what did you find?"

"Right there, on this one. Isn't it a flower?" Dahlia asked quizzically as she pointed to a very familiar grave.

I looked down to see one asphodel stem in full bloom. Entranced, my smile grew ever so big as well as tears welling up in my eyes.

"Mother, is it the flower you have been looking for?"

"Why are you crying if you are smiling?"

The children had so many questions, and I only had one answer.

"Yes, my darlings, this is the flower I was looking for, and you found it. Isn't it delightful?"

"Oh, I love it. The flower is as lovely as you." Robert added.

"So, if it is the asphodel, why are you crying?" Edward asked.

"Boys, before you two were born and Dahlia was just a small baby, this cemetery was filled with asphodels, but an accident happened and they burned away. I never thought I would see them again growing here. Now, I have hope."

Dahlia studied me and finally asked, "Isn't your name Asphodel?"

"It is and your grandfather named me after these charming flowers."

"So, that's why you are crying because this one came back?" Edward still wanted an answer.

"I am crying, yes, because one of them did come back, but I am crying more because this is my sister's grave it grew upon. Come here you three. I love you so." I decreed, hugging them all together, looking at Astra's gravestone and the asphodel thriving in front of it. It gave me a sense of love sent from my sister. She gave my life back to me when she saved me, she gave my two boys life when she saved me, and now she was giving me back my asphodels—maybe only one by one. Astra had her faults, but in the end, she put family first over herself. To thank her, I would make sure Dahila was loved and provided for the rest of her life. I would cherish this moment for the rest of my life.

"Boys, I have a task for you. Please go up to the shed and look for more tools like this one," I said as I held up a garden trowel.

"Yes, Mother, come on Edward. I'll beat you there." Robert instructed as they ran as fast as they could.

"Dahlia, sit down next to me, please."

"Mother, are you sure you are okay?"

"Yes, my darling, I need to tell you a story."

"Oh, is it the one about Rose-Red? I do love her personality and her red hair!"

"You could say that the girl I am about to tell you about is kind of like Rose-Red. She did have a fiery personality." I pointed to the tombstone as I began to tell Dahlia about Astra. "See this tombstone right here where you found the asphodel? As I said before, this was my sister, Astra."

"Oh Mother, she had a lovely name."

"Yes, she did. Astra and I were twins. That means that when your grandmother gave birth to us, we came into this world on the same day, together. We looked the exact same—hair, skin, height, and everything else. People who did not know us well had a hard time telling us a part, making us mirror images of one another. The only differences in us were our personalities. I am shy by nature, but Astra was a social butterfly. That means she was never afraid to talk to anyone, even if they were a stranger."

"Oh, she must have been a fun lady."

"Dahlia, she was, we loved each other, but we did bicker from time to time as siblings, especially as sisters do. When we were older, before you were born, Astra decided to get married and move away."

"Didn't she still like you?"

"Well, yes, but sometimes when ladies marry gentlemen, they must move to be with the gentleman's family."

"Oh, I see."

"We did not get to see Astra for several months, but then she came for a visit to see us. We were excited to see her; however, she was not by herself."

"Did she bring her husband?"

"No, he had lots of work to do, so she visited without him, but she brought her baby with her, a beautiful baby girl."

"Where is she now? I mean the little girl?"

"Darling Dahlia, that baby was you."

"I am not sure I get it."

"Dahlia, this may be hard for you to understand, but sometimes mothers and fathers bring babies into the world as their own, but sometimes they take in a baby from someone else because of different circumstances."

"So, you and Father took me to raise from Astra. The lady whose grave is right here. Your sister?"

"Yes, Astra loved you with all her heart. She was the proudest mother! She stayed with us quite a while because she missed us so and needed to be near her family. Before she returned home, your father and I had married. Not long after Astra came home, I found out I was going to have a baby."

"Were that baby Robert and Edward?"

"Yes, the babies were Robert and Edward. While we were waiting for them to arrive, one day I was out in the cemetery. You know how I like to sit on my bench."

"Oh yes! I love to sit with you there."

"I love for you to do that, too," I agreed brimming with joy as I hugged her before telling her the rest of the story, "Well, the grass was very dry that summer and somehow, we had a fire. I had fallen asleep and the flames were all around me. Astra had come outside and saw me. She rushed through the fire and pulled me out. Dahlia, she saved my life."

"She did that! Oh, how heroic she was."

"Yes, dear, she was. If Astra had not done that, neither I nor your brothers would be here today. Dahlia, she gave her life to save the three of us. She was the most heroic person I ever knew. I was waiting for the right time to tell you all of this. Today, when you found the asphodel, I felt it was a sign for me to tell you. I love you sweet child."

Dahlia stared at the tombstone, pondering in her little mind taking all of this in. It made me question whether I should have told her all of those things, and especially without Benjamin. After a few minutes, she moved her hand across Astra's name, and then gazed at the asphodel bloom below. She began to smile and looked up at me, "For her to think of you instead of herself means she was a beautiful, smart lady. I wish I could have known her. I hope you will tell me more stories about her."

"I will most definitely do that."

"I know she was my real mother, but I am going to still call you Mother because you are the only mother I have ever known and a lady like her would want me to call you that, especially since you said you two were two peas in a pod." Dahlia rationalized smiling.

"Speaking of peas, she did not like peas with a passion."

Giggling loudly, "I've never liked peas either."

We embraced each other as a loving mother and loving child do with a few tears in my eyes lingering. The boys had just come around a tombstone with the tool treasure I asked them to find.

"Mother, are you still crying? Why?" Edward was concerned.

"Darling, I am quite all right. I was sharing with Dahlia about a very important person in our lives she needed to know about."

"Robert and Edward, I will tell you about her sometime. She was just like Mother in every way. She was an asphodel—she was a forever flower and a loyal light.

Chapter 48

The next twenty years were spent in enormous bliss with my family. Benjamin and I still felt as newlyweds and always being there for each other *for the Spirit of Love reigneth and ruleth* in our house. Our children grew to be good humans who thrived in school as they studied, they participated in school activities, and even began learning the family business eagerly.

In 1890, my father passed away from heart disease. He struggled with the illness for five years, but finally gave up the ghost. His loss was felt strongly among all of us. We grieved for such a long time, I wearing mourning attire for longer than I expected to. Thomas Willoughby was a grand man who suffered from great losses throughout his life; however, the last fifteen or so years of his life, he spent with his grandchildren, soaking up their energy, knowing the future was bright where he was leaving a lasting legacy. Benjamin organized a funeral for the angels for my father—Benjamin's magnum opus. The heartfelt sentiments in every detail shown to all who attended. Everyone knew what a special man he was.

By 1899, Dahlia was married to a wonderful young man who treated her like a queen. Astra would be so proud of the young woman she had become. Dahlia had the spirit of Astra, but the persona of me—a blend of both of us Willoughby girls packed just right. Robert and Edward finished college and were back living with us and working side by side in now, Willoughby, Richardson, and Sons. Before Papa died, he insisted Benjamin add Richardson into the business name if Robert and Edward ever decided to make this a part of their lives.

At the beginning of January 1900, we had an incredibly harsh winter with more clients than we would ever expect. The reason for all this death—influenza. It was running rampant through our little town of Spencerton as if it had a quota to keep. Unfortunately, I succumbed to this illness.

Before the influenza attack on me, we were celebrating a wonderful family filled Christmas together. Dahlia and her husband, Perry, stayed with us through New Year's Day. Perry was a lawyer and needed to get back to his work. Dahlia favored Astra more than Alfred with her hair a slightly lighter shade of red almost strawberry blonde. Her eyes were more violet now she was older. She was the same height and build as her mother, but the only difference was she had Alfred's nose, which was more pronounced, but it was just right. Speaking of Alfred, we never heard from him again. Dahlia's husband Perry was over six foot tall with a muscular build; he had thick wavy black hair he smoothed back, and his eyes were steel gray. They made a handsome couple.

Robert and Edward took after Benjamin in every way. They were the same height with the same color of eyes. The only difference was they received a variation of my auburn hair, only slightly darker—brown with auburn gleaming when they were in the sun. We were both so proud of them and hoped now they were finished with school, and settled into the family business each one would find a wife.

During the holiday season by day, all the men were at work while Perry conducted his own business and paperwork so he would not get behind. Each night, we would have dinner, reminisce about old stories, and play games. We smiled and laughed more than ever before.

One evening before the sun was going down, I went to put out wreaths on the graves of my mother, father, Astra, and Benjamin's fathers. I placed my cloak over my shoulders, gathering my things. I always did this by myself. I enjoyed the quiet of the lingering sun disappearing as I would finish where I could speak to them peacefully alone. Benjamin would come out and see my handiwork on another day or evening.

As I finished, I looked up at the sky to see the twilight ambiance I loved so much. The stars were starting to make their appearance as guests dancing on the skies. Out of the corner of my eye, I saw someone whom I figured was one of my children. When I turned to them, I saw someone I had not seen in many moons ago. It was Berenice.

"Berenice, how are you? Where have you been?"

"Oh, Asphodel, I have been ill and so I do not come out too much. I had to see you though."

"I have missed you so. I thought you moved away and forgot to tell me."

"I am so sorry for disappearing. I have not been in the best spirits. My melancholy has been so strong."

Before I said anything else, I gazed upon her because something seemed unusual. I was in my mid-forties. While I still appeared not too old, showing my age, Berenice still looked as though we were teenagers. She even wore a similar dress she wore the last time I saw her. I guessed she was blessed to still appear so young; however, her face showed a great sadness.

"I am so sorry to hear you have been in such a state. I am so joyful to see you again. I do wish you the happiest new year. Hopefully, I will see you more often; maybe come for some tea."

"I will try for tea, but I know I will see you soon. You can count on that. Asphodel, be careful this time of year. You know how much sickness is around."

"Thank you, and please do the same. I mean, you be careful too."

"Well, I better go. The sun is almost down, and I better get back home out of the cold."

"Goodbye Berenice."

"I will see you soon, Asphodel. So long for now."

I stood for a minute more at my family's graves and turned to go inside; Berenice was gone. I always wondered how she went out of the cemetery so fast. As I was walking back towards the house, I felt warmth coming over me like a shadow hovering over a grave. I began to perspire, and unexpectedly suffered from a weakness all over. I picked up my pace to get back to the house as soon as I could. It took every ounce of energy to walk up the stairs into the kitchen. Winnie immediately saw me and grimaced. "Ma'am, what's wrong? Should I go get Mr. Benjamin?"

"Yes, Winnie…and hurry please."

The next thing I knew, I was in my bed dressed in my night-gown with the doctor finishing up his exam. It wasn't Dr. Haynes; it was now Dr. Jones. Dr. Haynes passed away ten years ago, and his grandson took up his practice. "Mrs. Richardson, let me go and get your husband so I can explain my diagnosis to both of you."

Dr. Jones left the room for just a moment, meaning Benjamin was waiting just outside the door. "I am afraid Mrs. Richardson has influenza. Her fever is high and growing higher. I will leave you with directions as to what to do for her. If she feels worse, please send for me immediately."

Benjamin looked at the doctor gravely and then at me. I thought I saw a tear rise up in his eye, but I was not quite sure. I was in such a daze I could have been dreaming. I heard Benjamin saying goodbye to the doctor and shut our door. "Asphodel, you have been in and out of sleep the past few hours. Did you hear what Dr. Jones explained?"

"Yes, dear. Let's do whatever he said."

The next few days were a blur. I had dreams of madness. Everyone I ever knew was in the dreams as if they were still alive. In between these fits, I could feel Benjamin's hand, I could see him and hear him. I could also see my children. I felt worse than the first day, but it did not seem as I was getting any better. My whole body went through strong bouts of heat and then cold to the extreme. I actually was not sure what day it was. I heard a different voice speaking to me, but it took me a few minutes to discern it was Dr. Jones again.

"Asphodel, it's Dr. Jones. I am going to reassess how you are doing."

"Yes, doctor."

He was with me for a little while, then I heard him speaking with a man on the other side of the room. I could finally make out it was Benjamin. I was so weak now, feeling as cold as I ever felt in my life. "Mother, it's Dahlia."

"Dahlia, I am so happy to hear your voice."

"Mother, save your energy, let me speak. I love you so much and we are praying for you every day to heal. I love you and always will."

A tear dropped onto my hand as warm as the ocean. I thought, why is she crying? "I love you too my child. You brought me so much joy. I love you with all my heart."

She hugged me with blubbering tears and then stepped away from the bed. Robert and Edward spoke to me after Dahlia. Where was Benjamin? What was going on? Was I dreaming again?

"Mother, please keep resting. We both just want to say a few words to you. You do not need to speak. Save your strength. You have been the most wonderful mother boys could ask for, especially for Edward and me. We know we were handfuls, but you gave us such grace and respect as we grew up. Mother, I love you so much." Robert stopped as his voice squeaked at the end of his sentence.

"It's me, Edward, Mother. Just like Robert said, you are the best mom a boy could have. I would not be the man I am now if it were not for you. From my whole heart, I love you!" Edward mimicked the same voice as Robert did and then I felt both of them hug me with bawling.

"Darling Asphodel, it is your Benjamin." I stopped him before he could say anything else.

"Benjamin, what is going on? Am I dying?" *She had seen that the finger of Death was upon her bosom — that, like the ephemeron, she had been made perfect in loveliness only to die.*

"The influenza is not getting any better, and your fever is higher than it should be. Dr. Jones is afraid you do not have very long in this world. He is not sure how long, but he knows death will come soon."

I contemplated what he said as best as I could with my mind so muddled by fever. The first tear surfaced like the first raindrop of a storm, and then the flood began. Benjamin began to speak, "Darling, if I could take this illness away, I would do it so quickly. You have been the heart and soul of my world. *I loved...[you]...with a love more fervent and more intense than I believed it possible to feel on earth.*" At his last words, he grabbed me up to him, embracing me as if he would never let me go.

"Oh Benjamin, say it isn't so. I never dreamed I would ever marry, but then you came along and turned my existence upside down," I paused to catch my breath as I stared into his elegant eyes of the clearest blue, "Not only did you give me love, but you also gave me children to love. They are the best thing we ever did together. Our love is not one of fairytales, our love is one of dramas brought on by real life, real passion, and real staying power. I wish for our children to experience that love." As I stopped for breath, I saw Berenice coming into the room, holding out her hand to me. "Berenice, you are so kind to come and see me. I am not long for this world."

Benjamin looked at me, wondering what I was saying, and saw me looking toward the door. "Asphodel, I know and that is why I am here. I am taking you with me."

"Benjamin, what is she saying. Where am I going?"

He was confused and responded, "Darling, you are staying right here with me and our children."

"But…Benjamin…she said she came to get me."

"Who said this?"

"My friend, Berenice."

Benjamin looked around, "Asphodel, it is just the two of us."

I gave a wry smile. Even in my feverish mind, I finally figured out my friend, Berenice. I never saw her anywhere but in the cemetery. She was a spirit who visited me, waiting for me to pass on into her world.

"Asphodel, it is time. I am so sorry." Berenice stated plainly.

"Darling, I must go. Hold onto my love for the end of time."

"Asphodel, please, my darling, I love you." Benjamin cried uncontrollably and held me with all of his strength.

"I will always love you Benjamin." I said as I hugged him as hard as I could, closing my eyes as I felt myself leaving my body, walking to Berenice as she guided me out of the room.

Journal entry of Benjamin Richardson dated June 21, 1900:

Dearest Asphodel,

Not a day goes by where I do not write to you. Today, I visited your grave on the last day of spring during the year you died. We buried you on the cold, bitter winter day, January 19, 1900. It was the hardest day I ever faced in my life because you were gone and never to return. Half of my light burned out the day you died; however, our children keep me alive, knowing a part of you lives on in them.

I also visit your grave every morning after breakfast. It keeps me close to you. This habit is one I have grown to love, and I have not missed a day coming to talk to you. Even on winter days filled with the ground brimming with snow, I still visited your grave. You are buried next to Astra. In life you were both born together; therefore, in death, you would be buried side by side.

As the days warmed and spring began on March 20th, it made it that much easier to walk outside. Robert and Edward help me with the cemetery grounds, keeping them up to par based on your standards. They always want to make sure you would not be disappointed if you gazed upon the grounds yourself.

This morning, I went outside for my morning constitutional through the cemetery straight to where my heart lies underground. Oh, I forgot to tell you, the boys placed a concrete bench by your grave so I could sit, making it easier for me to stay with you longer. Now, back to what I am so excited to tell you. When I arrived at your resting place, I began talking to you while I looked down at the ground. I noticed the asphodel on Astra's grave peeking through the dirt ready to spring up just as it had bloomed again after the fire. After seeing it, I looked over by your tombstone, and to my elated eyes did I see another asphodel making its presence.

> *— these spots, not less than the whole surface of the valley, from the river to the mountains that girdled it in, were carpeted all by a soft green grass, thick, short, perfectly even, and vanilla-perfumed, but so besprinkled throughout with the yellow buttercup, the white daisy, the purple violet, and the ruby-red asphodel, that its exceeding beauty spoke to our hearts in loud tones, of the love and of the glory of God.*

When you first saw the asphodel bloom on Astra's grave, it was like her giving a sign to you she was at peace. Since the one asphodel began blooming so many years ago, we have not seen another one. Then, to see this coming up from the ground lets me know you too are at peace, and not alone; you are with your sister. The bond you shared can never be unbroken—the asphodels are proof.

My beloved darling wife,
Never brought any strife.
As the sun shines down
O'er the fertile ground,
It brings warmth to two
As the bulbs rejuvenate anew.
They push up to see a new dawn
In front of tombstones on the lawn.
These are the only ones I need
As the rain upon them feeds,
Sprouting and blooming brave
Blossoms on your graves.
Mirror images born as one

With all of life done.
Two asphodels bonded here.
Two sisters so dear.
Even if no more flowers grow,
My one asphodel will always know
My love for her heretofore
Shall cease *nevermore*.

Asphodel, my darling, I love you. As for tomorrow, I will speak to you again.

Your beloved,

Benjamin

About the Author

Carmen Bouldin works as an English teacher—working in education since 2004. In her spare time, she writes gothic romance, mystery, and poetry. Much of her writing and art is inspired by Edgar Allan Poe. Her debut novella, *The Rose Bush*, was published May 16, 2025. It is the first book in her Gothic Garden Series. Her poem, "The Raven's Mourning," was nominated for a Saturday Visiter Award in 2020. This poem was published in Raven's Quoth Press' poetry anthology, *Evermore 4*, in 2024. She also has poems in the Raven's Quoth Press' poetry anthologies *Cherish 2* and *Evermore 5*. She cohosts a podcast, The Six Degrees of Edgar A. Poe, where she and her POEcast partner, Jeanie Smith, discuss Poe's influences on multiple genres. She also enjoys creating visual art. Her painting, "There's no Place like Poe," was nominated for a Saturday Visiter Award in 2019. A native Memphian, Carmen, resides in Middle Tennessee with her husband, Jeff, and their three cats, solid black cat-Poe, tuxedo cat-Montresor, and solid black cat-Forunato. Carmen and Jeff love to travel and wear vintage inspired attire Carmen creates through the art of sewing.

You may find Carmen's writing, art, and sewing at the following:

Website: https://thequotableraven.com/

Facebook - @thequotableraven

X - @thequoteraven

Instagram - @thequotableraven

Instagram - @ravenmade23

You may find Carmen and Jeanie's POEcast at:

www.sixdegreesofpoe.com

Facebook – @the6degreesofedgarallanpoe

X – @sixdegreesofpoe

Instagram – @sixdegreesofpoe

Spotify –
https://open.spotify.com/show/09UNSDV4ZXIEf19ZhQwJ63?si=49fa62b4329441ba

YouTube - https://www.youtube.com/@poeunplugged3978